Robert Smith

Poems of Controversy Betwixt Episcopacy and Presbytery

also several poems and merry songs on other subjects. With some funeral elegies

on various noblemen and gentlemen

Robert Smith

Poems of Controversy Betwixt Episcopacy and Presbytery
also several poems and merry songs on other subjects. With some funeral elegies on various noblemen and gentlemen

ISBN/EAN: 9783337180195

Printed in Europe, USA, Canada, Australia, Japan

Cover: Foto ©Andreas Hilbeck / pixelio.de

More available books at **www.hansebooks.com**

INTERESTING COLLECTIONS

OF

𝕭allad 𝕻oetry, etc.

PUBLISHED OR SOLD BY

THOMAS GEORGE STEVENSON,

Antiquarian and Historical Bookseller,

22 FREDERICK STREET, EDINBURGH,

(At the Sign of Sir Walter Scott's Head).

"Whose Shop is well known, or ought to be so, by all the true lovers of curious little old smoke=dried volumes."

Chambers's Illustrations of the Author of Waverley.

Ballad-Books: FOUR BOOKS OF CHOICE OLD SCOTISH BALLADS, viz. :— I. A BALLAD-BOOK. — II. A NORTH COUNTRIE GARLAND. — III. THE BALLAD-BOOK ; and, IV. A NEW BOOK OF OLD BALLADS. Edited originally by CHARLES KIRKPATRICK SHARPE, JAMES MAIDMENT, and GEORGE RITCHIE KINLOCH. *Now First Collected.* Sm. 8vo, *woodcut portraits of the Accomplished Antiquary,* CHARLES KIRKPATRICK SHARPE, *and* CHARLES LESLIE, *alias* "*Mussel Mou'd Charlie, the Celebrated Ballad-Singer in Aberdeen,*" &c. Boards. 30s. 1868

*** "ONLY ONE HUNDRED AND FIFTY-FIVE COPIES OF THIS VERY REMARKABLE COLLECTION PRINTED."

Smith (Robert, School-Master at Glenshee), POEMS OF CONTROVERSY betwixt EPISCOPACY and PRESBYTERY : Being the Substance of what past 'twixt him and several other Poets ; as also SEVERAL POEMS and MERRY SONGS on other subjects ; with some FUNERAL ELEGIES on several Noblemen and Gentlemen. *Reprinted from the Edition of* 1714. Sm. 8vo, *boards*. 1869

☞ " This very odd Miscellany—a mixture of Satires, Elegies, Mirth, and Sadness, penned on several subjects and occasions,—has long been a work of EXTREME RARITY."

*** " THE IMPRESSION HAS BEEN LIMITED TO SEVENTY COPIES, FOR SUBSCRIBERS ONLY."

Williams's (Sir Charles Hanbury) Poetical Works. With Notes and Illustrations, by HORACE WALPOLE, *Earl of Orford.* Edited, with a Preface, by LORD HOLLAND. 3 vols. Sm. 8vo, *portraits, boards*. 10s. 6d. 1822

☞ " Perfect specimens of the most keen and irresistible satire."

Kinloch's Ancient Scottish Ballads. Recovered from Tradition, and *never before published ;* with Notes, Historical and Explanatory, and an Appendix containing the *Airs of several of the Ballads.* Sm. 8vo, *boards*. 10s. 6d. 1827

☞ " The Editor of this Collection has judiciously abstained from all conjectural emendations, and presented to the public, in the shape he received them, a considerable number of Traditionary Ballads, principally obtained from recitation in the Northern Shires."—WILLIAM MOTHERWELL.

" Various valuable Collections of Ancient Ballad Poetry have appeared of late years, some of which are illustrated with learning and acuteness :—those of Mr. Motherwell and of Mr. Kinloch intimate much taste and feeling for this species of literature."—SIR WALTER SCOTT.

Kelly (Thomas, Sixth Earl of): MINUETS, SONGS, &c., Composed by,—*now for the first time published*, with an Introductory Notice, by CHARLES KIRKPATRICK SHARPE. 4to, *portrait and plates, boards*. 10s. 6d. 1839

☞ " The compositions of this very eminent musical genius were celebrated by his contemporaries, and ought still to be esteemed as an honour to Scotland. He was one of the finest musical composers of the age."

*** " ONLY SIXTY COPIES PRINTED."

Scotish Elegiac Verses on the Principal Nobility and Gentry of Scotland, from 1629 to 1729 ; with Interesting Biographical Notices, Notes, and an Appendix of Illustrative Papers, by JAMES MAIDMENT. Sm. 8vo, *boards*, 10s. 6d.   1842

> ☞ " The FUNERAL POEMS collected in this volume, although deficient in poetical merit, deserve preservation, as adding some by no means unimportant additions to our store of Historical and Biographical information. They have been printed from copies *many of them unique*."

> ** "A CURIOUS AND INTERESTING COLLECTION, DESERVING OF EVERY NOTICE."

Buchanan (George), Epithalamium on the Marriage of FRANCIS and MARY QUEEN OF SCOTS. Translated from the Original. 8vo, *stitched*. 2s.   1845

> ** " IMPRESSION LIMITED TO SIXTY-FIVE COPIES."

Ayrshire Ballads and Songs. Illustrated with Sketches, Historical, Traditional, Narrative, and Biographical, by JAMES PATERSON, with Remarks by CAPT. GRAY. 8vo, *boards*. 5s. 6d.   1846–47

> ☞ " This Selection is curious and good, and no lover of Scottish Songs ought to be without a copy. The illustrative Notes and Sketches are highly interesting, and serve to throw considerable light on the ballad lore of the West."

Dalyell's (Sir John Graham) Musical Memoirs of Scotland. With Historical Annotations and Notes, illustrative of the MANNERS AND CUSTOMS OF SCOTLAND, &c. 4to, *embellished with 45 plates, boards*. 42s.   1849

> ☞ " This singularly curious and highly interesting work treats chiefly of those instruments which are recognised in Scotland, with Dissertations on the ' Bagpipe, Ecclesiastical Ornaments, Modern Performance, the Organ, Wind Instruments, Springs, Bells, Stringed Instruments, Guitar, Lute, Harp, Instruments with Keys, &c."

> " Mr. Laing in his " *Introduction* to Stenhouse's Illustrations of the Lyric Poetry and Music of Scotland," remarks that ' The Title of this Volume furnishes no very distinct notion of its contents, which exhibit the result of a long-continued and laborious investigation into the History of Music in Scot-

land, selected from copious collections on the subject of Scottish History, the accumulations of many years, and accompanied with plates of the various Musical Instruments in use from the earliest dates.' "

** " ONLY TWO HUNDRED AND FIFTY COPIES PRINTED."

Renfrewshire Poets: The POEMS of the SEMPILLS OF BELTREES, viz. :—I. The Packman's Paternoster ; or, A Picktooth for the Pope.—II. The Life and Death of Habbie Simson, Piper of Kilbrachan.—III. Epitaph on Sanny Briggs.—IV. The Banishment of Poverty.—V. A Discourse between Law and Conscience.—VI. The Blythsome Wedding.—VII. She raise and loot me in.—VIII. Maggie Lauder. *Now first Collected*, with Notes, Biographical Notices of their Lives, and an Appendix of Illustrative Documents, by JAMES PATERSON. Sm. 8vo, *boards*. 10s. 6d.   1849

☞ " The Sempills of Beltrees are distinguished by a kind of heriditary affiance to letters and the muses ; and various eminently successful effusions have been ascribed to individuals of the family. There can be no doubt that a careful collection of their poetical writings, accompanied with memoirs of the writers, would prove highly acceptable and useful to Scottish literature."

" A deserved compliment is thus paid to a family distinguished for genius. And valuable as a contribution to the general literary history and biography of the country, for which the reader of Scottish poetry, especially the lover of what is old, cannot fail to be grateful."

** " ONLY TWO HUNDRED AND FIFTY COPIES PRINTED."

Hamilton (William, of Bangour) Poems and Songs of, Collated with the MSS., and containing several pieces *hitherto unpublished ;* including the Original Prefaces by Dr. ADAM SMITH and LORD ESKGROVE; with an Introductory Notice, Illustrative Notes, and an Account of the Life of the Author, by JAMES PATERSON. 12mo, *portraits, boards.* 5s.   1850

☞ " He may be reckoned among the earliest of the Scotch Poets who wrote English verse with propriety and taste. We think, therefore, that Mr. Paterson has done good service in producing a new edition of a Scottish Poet, who can still please or interest his countrymen. No pains have been spared to perfect the work. Mr. David Laing has contributed to its pages from his manuscript collections: and Mr. Charles Kirkpatrick Sharpe has drawn upon his memory to enrich its notes and illustrations."

" The poems of the elegant and amiable Hamilton of Bangour, display regular design, just sentiments, fanciful invention, pleasing sensibility, elegant diction, and smooth versification. The truly beautiful ballad of the ' Braes of Yarrow,' has been almost universally acknowledged to be one of the finest ever written, and would alone have immortalised his name."

Maidment's Scotish Ballads and Songs   With an Introductory Notice and Illustrative Notes.   12mo, *boards.* 10s. 6d.   1859

☞ " This interesting collection consists of curious, old, rare, unique Ballads and Songs, which are *not to be found in any other collection*, with a few from MSS., NOW FOR THE FIRST TIME PRINTED.—The Introductory Notes afford much valuable information."

Lithgow (William, the Celebrated Scotish Traveller):
POETICAL REMAINS, 1618–1660.—I. The Pilgrimes Farewell, to his Natiue Countrey of Scotland, 1618.—II. Scotland's Teares in his Countreyes behalf, 1625.—III. Scotland's Welcome to her Native Sonne, and Soveraigne Lord, King Charles, 1633.—IV. The Gushing Teares of Godly Sorrow, 1640.—V. A Briefe and Summarie Discourse upon that lamentable and dreadfule disaster at Dunglasse, 1640.—VI.— Scotland's Parænesis to her dread Soveraign King Charles the Second, 1660.   NOW FIRST COLLECTED, and Edited, with Bibliographical Notices by JAMES MAIDMENT.   Sm. 4to, *boards.* 30s.   1863

*** " THIS COLLECTION OF EXCEEDINGLY RARE AND INTERESTING POEMS WAS PRINTED CHIEFLY FOR SUBSCRIBERS, AND THE IMPRESSION LIMITED TO ONE HUNDRED COPIES."

Black-Letter Ballads and Broadsides: A Collection of SEVENTY-NINE, printed during the Reign of Queen Elizabeth, between the years 1559 and 1597. Edited with an Introduction and Illustrative Notes by HALLIWELL. Sm. 8vo, *boards.* 12s.   1867

☞ " All of the highest interest and curiosity, presumed to be unique, and hitherto unknown."

Percy's (Bishop) Folio Ballad Manuscript: BALLADS AND ROMANCES, with LOOSE AND HUMOROUS SONGS. Edited with Illustrative Notes and Introduction, by HALES and FURNIVALL, assisted by CHILD and CHAPPELL. 3 vols. 8vo, *half-bound, uncut.* 42s.   1867–68

☞ " The reader is here presented with Select Remains of our ancient English Bards and Minstrels, printed from the rare original FOR THE FIRST TIME IN A COMPLETE UNMUTILATED FORM. As a mere piece of printing—a mass of paper and type—the PERCY BALLADS are wonderfully cheap, and the work is certain to become scarce before long."

Surgundo; or, The Valiant Christian: A METRICAL HISTORY of the Feuds and Conflicts of the GORDON FAMILY. Edited from the Original Manuscript, with Illustrative Notes by CHARLES KIRKPATRICK SHARPE. 4to, *portrait and plates, boards.* 10s. 6d.   1837

₊ " ONLY FIFTY COPIES PRINTED CHIEFLY FOR PRESENTS."

The Gude and Godlie Ballates: A COMPENDIOUS BOOK OF PSALMS AND SPIRITUAL SONGS, commonly known as "The Gude and Godlie Ballates." *Reprinted from the Edition of* 1578. Edited, with an Introductory Notice, Illustrative Notes, and a Glossary, by DAVID LAING. 12mo, *boards.* 10s. 6d.   1868

☞ " This 'Compendious Book' should properly be regarded as a POETICAL MISCELLANY by various authors. The flowers it exhibits may not be remarkable either for poetical fragrance or beauty, although variegated both as to form and colour. But whatever estimate we may form of the Collection, it has its own peculiar value, in connexion with the literature of the Reformation period in Scotland ; and being the only one of its kind, this little volume deserves to be better known than it is at the present day."

₊ " ONLY THREE HUNDRED AND FIFTY COPIES PRINTED."

Sempill Ballads, 1567-1573: A Collection of Curious and Interesting SCOTISH HISTORICAL AND POLITICAL BALLADS, by ROBERT SEMPILL. (*Originally Printed in Black-Letter, at Edinburgh, as separate Broadsides.*)—NOW FIRST COLLECTED.—*Preparing for Publication.*

Robert Smith's

Controversial Poems,

Merry Songs, and Funeral Elegies.

M.DCC.XV.

POEMS

OF

CONTROVERSY

BETWIXT

Episcopacy and Presbytery:

ALSO SEVERAL

POEMS AND MERRY SONGS ON OTHER
SUBJECTS.

WITH SOME

FUNERAL ELEGIES ON VARIOUS
NOBLEMEN AND GENTLEMEN.

By ROBERT SMITH,

School-Master at Glenshee, Perthshire.

Edinburgh:

Reprinted from the Original Edition of 1714.

M.DCCC.LIII.

R. Syme & Son, Printers, Edinburgh.

To the Courteous Reader.

IN submitting to your notice a NEW EDITION of the "Poems of Controversy betwixt Episcopacy and Presbytery: (*never before published*) by ROBERT SMITH, *Schoolmaster at Glenshee*, Printed in the year 1714," I have to remark that with respect to the Compiler or the Authors of this Collection, it has not been in my power to discover any additional particulars, beyond what are to be gleaned from a perusal of this work, as to their Parentage, Birth, Religious, Political, or Professional Character and Habits, or even as to the dates of their deaths.

This very odd Miscellany,—"a mixture of Satyrs, Elogies, Mirth and Sadness, pen'd on several subjects and occasions"—has long been a work of considerable scarcity, and in much request among Collectors of old Scotish Poetry. In it are to be found one or two Poems of no inconsiderable pretensions, but in language, which if used by Dominies of the present day, would certainly excite some commotion in quiet rural parishes.

As a proof of its GREAT RARITY, NO COPY of this volume is to be found in any of those large and rich Bibliographical Stores, the Libraries of the University, Faculty of Advocates, or the Writers to the Signet, in this city. In a Catalogue of Books published by Mr. Thomas Thorpe, London, in 1843, there appeared a copy, the price of which was marked Two Guineas. There is a copy in the fine library of the late SIR WALTER SCOTT at Abbotsford, near Melrose. DAVID LAING, Esq. (of this city), possesses another, which, I believe, was formerly in the library of the late PRINCIPAL JOHN LEE. And a third is to be found in that of the Free Church College, Edinburgh. The copy last referred to has several *corrections* in Manuscript which appear to have been made before the volume was issued; and affixed at the end is a PRINTED ADDITION of an Address to " WILLIAM SETON, *Younger of Pitmedden.*" These emendations and addition, distinguishable by being printed within Brackets [   ], I have retained so as to make the Collection as perfect as possible.

A wish to gratify a few friends and patrons, who are enthusiastic Collectors of Scotish Ballad Poetry, is the sole inducement for making this FACSIMILE REPRINT. The number of Copies is strictly limited to SEVENTY, for Subscribers only.

T. G. S.

EDINBURGH, 1869.

S M I T H's
P O E M S

O F

C O N T R O V E R S Y

B E T W I X T

𝕰𝔭𝔦𝔰𝔠𝔬𝔭𝔞𝔠𝔶 and 𝔓𝔯𝔢𝔰𝔟𝔶𝔱𝔯𝔶:

Being the Substance of what past
'twixt him and several other Poets;

As also,

Several Poems and Merry Songs on
other Subjects:

With some Funeral Elegies on several
Noblemen and Gentlemen.

In two Parts.

By *Robert Smith* School-master at *Glenshee.*

---

*Never before **Published.***

Printed in the Year 1714.

TO THE

WORLD.

THE most part of *Mankind being Ambiti-ous to be in the favour of the great,* makes my *Ambition of the Superlative Degree, in seeking to find a great Patron for the following Piece.* 'Tis therefore, O Great World, *since thou art a Compound of Vanity, (and a* Jupiter *for greatness,) I have pre-sented thee with this Child in thy own Likeness, it being the worthless off-spring of one that is sprung of thee ; it being so like thy self, I could not in Justice Dedicate it to any other.*

Tho' I have chosen thee, a great Patron, yet sure I am, I cannot say, I have found thy large and Bounteous Liberality Manifested to me, what I get is from the Divine Hand, and there-fore I render thee no Thanks.

Tho' I seek thy right side, I am sure to find the wrong : Thou hast more Faces than Janus, *and Eyes than* Argus, *and 'tis as easie to get out of* Dedalus Labyrinth, *as to please thee ; and as there are few that pleaseth thee, so there are as few that are pleased with thee.*

'Tis [true], thou art that great Idol loved by All, but spoken good of by none : For my own part, I have little or no Cause to speak good of thee,

and

and far less to love thee, but among the number of my other Enemies.

The most part of Mankind, whom thou smiles upon with a Joabs Dissimulation, and a Judas Kiss; 'Tis only to cheat them out of more than thou can give them, or make their end worse than their beginning: They court thee with Carefulness, keep thee with Diligence, and are forced to part with thee for the Remorse of a too late Repentance.

Indeed we oftentimes pretend to hate thee, but 'tis because thou loves not us; But when we come to be try'd by the Touch-stone of Death, then we Manifest our Love to thee, by our loathness to leave thee: But this Unwillingness proceeds from a fear the next be worse than thou, or from the too great likeing we had to thee, in the short Days of our uncertain Pilgrimage.

I expect but little or no favour from thy greatest Votaries, whom thou hast made thy Chamberlains, who will (rather than part with a little of thy Gold) Starve and Damn themselves, in Purchassing Magnificent Estates to their Eldest Sons, which perhaps some of them will exhaust and expend in making an Union betwixt their Souls and the Cooling Grapes of Spain, and at last fall a Sacrifice to Bacchus Immortal Deity: On whose Tombs this Inscription may be Inserted,

The

The Fathers Liv'd in Miserie,
The Sons they Swim'd in Bowls :
The first were Damn'd for Knaverie,
The Latter Drank their Souls.

I intend to present none such with a Copy of my Book: But in spight of thee, O Great Idol, *there are some* Atholick *Spirits, who* **Live above the Allurements of thy smile, and affrightments of thy frowns, who are the well-wishers of** Apollo, **whose Hearts are neither joined to thee, nor become Baggs for thy rusty Gold :** *'Tis from such that I expect Friendship, because I have seen that once Glorious* Parnassus, *where* Apollo *was wont to be Venerat ; Though my feeble Strength was never able to climb that Glorious Mountain, nor take a full Draught of it's Superaboundant Sweet Water, whose streams are less hurtful (but more Healthful) to Mortals, than the purest Blood of the finest Grapes ; for it neither makes them have sore* Heads, Sick Hearts, *nor empty* Pockets ; *for there are few that are Liberal to Poets.*

O World, **thou hast for the present, cast my Lot far from the Muses Plowmen, and those who are, and have been Exercised, in those Glorious Fields and Delectable Soil of the Garden of** Apollo.

But in spight of thee, I have that which will keep me in mind of the Renowned Parnassus, *to wit,*

wit, the High bending and Sky kissing Moun-
tains of Athol, *whose Illustrious Prince may*
be Termed, The Mirror of Mankind, and
the Darling of Humane Race, *in whose*
Praise, none can commit an Hypervole ; whose
Seraphick Soul soars far above the Love of thee
(O World,) he is too Wise to be Tempted with
thy Vanity, or blinded by thy Gold ; he's a
Lover of Apollo, *but none of* Bacchus *Vo-*
taries, and may be called the Poets Patron, and
the Muses Friend :

A Prince (most Great) of many Lands and Hills, ⎫
From whose High Tops the Silver sand distills ; ⎬
His Noble Soul each Noble Virtue fills.   ⎭

He is such a Friend to the Muses, that if e-
very one according to their Respective Stations
were like him, the Poets *would once more throng*
Parnassus, *and Flourish their colours upon its*
once Glorious, but now Deserted Tops ; and
Inhib Lively draughts of the Heleconian *Foun-*
tain ; The way to which is scarcely sought for,
by the Discouraged Spirits of this Age.
Thou deals to the Poets for the most part with
a scrimp Hand, tho' to others with a Bountyful
Arm : Thou deserves their Satyrs, better than
their Elogies ; their Hatred, rather than Love ;
thou was excluded out [*of*] C—ts *Prayer, and shall*
never share of the small Praise that my Tongue
or Pen is capable of.

Tho'

The Epistle Dedicatory.

Tho' I have Dedicate the following piece to thee, yet I am sure to meet with least Friendship from thy nearest Relations, and greatest Lovers, they'll never give me so much as will pay the Printer, nor consider Paper Taxations: However, this is the Touchstone and Characteristical mark to know thy Friends from my own.

If any think I savour too much of Love to thee, let them blame the Printer, who will readily tell you, that all Trades must Live.

I come now, O World, to make my Apologie for presenting thee with the following Peice, thy own likeness as to the part of Vanity: When I Wrote the same, it was never in my Thought that it should be Exposed to the Publick view of thy harsh Criticks; but being advised by some, tho' none of thy Lovers, and considering Democritus can laugh, as well as Momus can carp, I have therefore sent it to thee and them; part among you, for one shall not have all.

Lanch forth, Lanch forth, into the World my Muse,
And for thy Master *Robin* plead excuse,
Who lives among the Mountains of *Glenshee*,
But had far rather sometimes be with thee:
Go search & try the World where e're thou finds,
Atholick Spirits, or kind Stralochlike minds.
Go now distinguish Misers from Good-fellows,
And know thy Masters Friends in great *Apollo's.*
To such I send thee for a Recreation,
Whom Fame Reports the Darlings of the Nation.
And if ye smile upon my Rustick strain,
I may hereafter come to Write again.
Glenshee Decr.
    15th. 1713.   *Robert Smith.*

TO THE

READER,

Candid Reader,

*S*IR Philip Sidney, *that admirable Orator and
Learned Poet, (in his Defence of Poetry) may
serve to justifie that excellent Art and pleasant
way of Writing, call'd Poetry: Tho' most part of the
Men of this Generation (as was noted long since)
takes that word* Poet, *for either Lover or Liar; He
answers many Objections and Aspersions that were laid
against Poetry and Poets, and proves its Excel-
lency from Reason and Antiquity: As any may read
in the fore-cited place.*

*But I have heard some Objections, that I hardly
think ever entred into his Brain, that any would show
their folly so far, as once to mention them.*

*The first Objection is, That all Poets have Bees in
their Heads. To which I Answer, That where there
are many Bees, there is some Honey, for without Honey they'll instantly die. Let any consider the Nature
of Bees they'll find they are Laborious Creatures, and
can suck Honey from the bitterest Flower of the Field.
But I would have such Gentlemen consider, that their
Heads must surely be as full of Drons, who can find
no sweetness in the Muses Well, nor Pleasure in the
Heliconian Hills. I truly think those Dronaticks find
a sweetness in nothing but in what pleases their Tastes*

A

To the Reader.

As one did once at a Feast find such sweetness in a Pockt-Pudding, which made him eat so largely, till his Throat was forc'd to give egression to the super-flous Guests of his Belly, and that on such a sudden, that those who came last in, went first out, they made such hurly burly striving for the Door, that he could have wish'd his Throat to have been as big as his Belly, at that time. Others stiles them Light in the Head. But I would be very glade if those Gentlemen would explain their Terms, whether they mean Lux *or* Le-vitas? *If the former, their Brains or Heads were the first things made in the Creation, He said,* Let there be Light and there was Light, *if it be this Light, then he that has Light in the Head is very happy, for Heaven it self is Emblemated and holden forth by Light: Yea moreover if the Opinion of the Philoso-phers holds true, that the Head is the Seat of the Soul, (none can deny that the Soul is an Heavenly Sub-stance, consequently Light) Then he that is not Light in Head hardly deserves the Name of a Man, be-cause he is* sine Anima. *But if the latter, viz.* Le-vitas, *Then they must grant that* omne Corpus leve ascendit, vel Naturaliter, vel Attractione; *If Natu-rally, then they do but seek or tend to their Center, from whence they came: If by Attraction, then they must be by some Superior and Over-ruling Power astricted and drawn to some loftier and more excellent Con-templation than many of those Block-heads, who are so ready to spit out their harmless Gall against them.*

This Art is spoken evil of by none, but by those, who are ignorant of it themselves: It were the hight of folly in me, to say that a Lawyer is Crack-brain'd, because he can Answer to every Point, and solve every Objection ex tempore *at the Bar, because I am*

B   *not*

not able to do the like: I think it no less folly in some who can hardly subscribe their own Names, to pass harsh Sentiments on Poets and their Works: Since ever I could decern a Pretty Man from a Block-head, I never heard any of Understanding and Learning speak ill of Poets qua Poets ; No doubt they have their other failings as others have, Though many of them were unskilfull, 'tis but a small matter, because they seek nothing for their Pains. And 'tis as rare to find any who gives them any, as to find a Hermophradite or an Unicorn: Tho' a Satyre rightly composed has often had as much influence to Reform a Wicked Man, as some cold Preachings.

For my own part, I deserve not to be among the Number of those whom I am vindicating; I will willingly stand at the foot of Helicon, and serve those who have drunk of the Pyrenian Well; Because my Ear hath been often penetrated with the sweet Echoes of their Melodious Strains.

Some are pleas'd to honour me with the Name of Poet, but no thanks to them, because 'tis out of Derision ; others attribute the same to me, Because I Love the Muses: But I am very far below that Name, I could wish I were one : It was once reckoned amongst the Properties of a Learned and Mighty King, his being a Poet ; and now it is thought folly, and the down-right sign of a Mad-man by the Sapient Blockheads of this Age: And yet themselves are so mad as to sing the Psalms of David Paraphras'd by a Quorum of these Mad-med, as themselves commonly term them.

Reader, *In the following Rustick Strain, thou hast a mixture of Satyrs, Elogies, Mirth, and Sadness, Pen'd on several Subjects and Occasions, None of which Satyrs were written without Ground and Provocation*

cation: Bitterness I suppose will seem to thee the greatest fault, But festring Wounds need nipping Salves, and great Crimes severe Rebukes.

Candid Reader, If thou be a Lover of Poesie (no doubt thou will be a Friend to Poets) I beg thy favourable Censer, I hope thou will rather mend my Errors, than dispise the Art for my sake, who am unskilful therein: But if thou be a Despiser of such Work-men and their Labours, I value thy Censer less than thou can do my verse, I remain thine as thou art mine.

Robert Smith.

B 2   A

A

POEM *on the Building of the School-house of* Glenshee.

L Ately at the Revolution,
 The World turn'd to that Condition,
 That from the King they took the Crown,
 And from the Bishops pull'd the Gown
To set them by as Idle Drons
Advanceing Presbyterian Tons,
Esteeming them no more than Fools,
Giving their Rents for to keep Schools.
 Duke *Athol* loving Piety,
A Hundred Merks got to *Glenshee.*
To some young Man to teach their youth :
Because their Fathers had such Drouth
Spending their Money in Abuses,
Rather than on Pious Uses ;
Some spending all at Dyce and Cards,
Some would rake Hell for to be Lairds ;
Sparing neither to oppress,
The Widow nor the Fatherless ;
Some Gluttons, some Tobacco-smoakers,
And most at sacred things were Mockers,
And some were Drunkards haunting Whores ;
And other some were Cheats and Liars :
They of their young Ones took no Care,
To give them either School or Lair.
 Our Gentles Learning doth appear,
By this that they can kill a Deer ;
And take Fish in forbidden time,
Althongh by Law it be a Crime.   To

To go about I am not stark ;
I'll return to the hunder Merk,
Which the Queen granted to *Glenshee*,
For to maintain a Dominie,
　This made the Lords [Lairds] a Tryst to hold,
That they might get a Fellow bold,
Then they resolved one to Call,
Out of the Colledge *Marishall ;*
One who hath Greek, and Latin speaks,
They are so large, they may be Dyks,
We'll have our Children Educat
And make them fit for Church and State.
　The Lad was call'd, a Tryst was held
At *Kerrow* there a School to Build :
They first resolv'd to spend the Summer
In bringing home Bridge-trees and Timber ;
To make every passage clear
Through all the Country far and near.
But I may fitly them compare,
Unto the wanton Grasshopper ;
That all the Summer idle Flees,
For they were so with their Bridge-trees.
　The Summer past, the Harv'st did come,
The Bridge-trees yet came never home,
And very few who hath a Peat,
Their Wives or Children for to heat :
He's thought a Man of no Repute,
Who hath a Clod to warm his Feet.
　The School-house yet was never Build,
Another Council must be held,
Yet they concluded it was best,
Their Corns first to put to rest.
　The Dominie greatly did fear,
They did intend his Eye to Blear ;
Yet he his Patience did extend,
Till it was worn to ane end,　　　　Then

Then after Reading he did say,
Unto them on a Sabbath-Day.
    My dear Friends, and all Well-wishers
You Heritors, and all Black Fishers
You Forresters, and all Deer killers,
Browsters, Husbandmen, and Millers,
I Pray you all give ear to me,
Christian Brethren of *Glenshee*,
It is well known unto you all,
At first from you I got a call,
For to come here to teach a School,
And now ye've us'd me as a Fool:
Having no place where to abide,
Nor any hole my head to hide,
But holds me wandering up and down,
As those who beg from Town to Town,
I have no constant place to stay,
Neither know I where to ly,
I hope ye'll have Consideration,
And Build my House from the Foundation,
Or else I will be forc'd to dwell,
Where ever Fortune doth me call,
    Thus having said, he made a halt,
And every one confest his fault.
    Then Old *Tom* to the rest did say,
My Friends, I do appoint *Friday*,
At *Kerrow* for to big the School,
For we'll no longer play the Fool.
    All from *Balno*, unto *Stronlyn*,
I pray you keep this Day in mind,
    Finningand and *Coridon*,
I pray you think this Day upon,
Dalmunzie, Leanoch-Muir and *Binzean*
With all the People of *Dalhinzean*,
Let all be-west the *Spittel* come,
And join your selves both *Cams* and *Tom*,   Ye

Ye People of *Bruchderge* and *Cray*,
Enderridries and *Rinavey ;*
Come all: For *Kerrow* he'll be there,
Waiting you when ye appear.
Thursday and Wednesday before
The Master went from Door to Door,
As any Beggar that doth thigg,
Intreating them his House to bigg.

   Every one did promise well,
To come for to Rear up the School.
The Day appointed had some frost,
They all keep't home their Shins to Rost:
They said let Schools go as they please,
We'll stay at home and take our ease.

   Yea *Tom* himself, who set the Day,
Went to *Braemar* to take his Play,
With *Kerrow* and his own Son *James*,
To fish upon *Glenclunies* streams ;
As likeways for to Hunt the Deer,
If any of them did appear.

   They spended there three Nights and Days,
Till they themselves were almost Preys
To Captain *Grant ;* who did them seek,
And made them almost file their breek.

   Says *Kerrow* though we be two Lairds
Yet we must run, for here are Guards,
Who will us either Head or Hang
Alas ! it's but a silly fange ;
The Devil take you all black Fish
Ye're like to prove a fatal Dish.

   O *Tom* since ye are best acquaint,
With th' Captain and the Laird of *Grant*,
I pray truse up what we have here,
For my part I dare not appear ;
For if they get me once but tean
They'll have me down to *Aberdeen*   And

And cast me into the Tolbooth
They will do that, alas forsooth
I know not to what hand to turn
I think I will run up the burn.

   Tears and sweat were on his Cheeks,
And worse I fear was in his Breeks,
They with the Wind did cast a smell
Which fear did from his Tripes expell,
His Eyes appear'd like Flames of Fire,
He being mov'd with fear and ire,
Again he turn'd as pale as Death,
And many a gasp gave, seeking Breath:
I wish I'd time to tell the story,
He needed no *memento mori ;*
At's Mouth were ball's like Water foam,
And thus he left his Neighbour *Tom,*

   Who being surpriz'd to see the People,
He stood as still as *Brechans* steeple,
And Prayers made to all the Saints
That they might pacifie the *Grants ;*
He unto all the Gods did call,
Sent *Mercury* to *Invercal,*
For to Solicitate *Dalmore*
Although they were at odds before ;
That he with *Grant* might interceed
To make him free from *Pisciceed.*

   O *Invercald,* ye's get a Deer,
As good's ye saw this seven year ;
Alas Sir I'm your Flesh and Blood,
Have Pity on me in my need ;
Alas who will give me relief,
But ye, my Name-sake, Friend and Chief :
For I's be no worse than my word,
Or let me Die upon a Sword,
If ever I Meat or Drink do spend
Till to your Gate a Deer I send.   He

He took his Gun, he dight his Eyen
And pour'd the Water out of his Sheen,
He up the brae right fast did prick,
When at the top through his Prospect
He looked round, both far and near
If he could spy a good fat Deer.
He presently a Flock did spy,
Advancing to him speedily;
He thought that did Prognosticat
He was a man belov'd of fate.

Then he upon his Knees did stay,
Not Worshipping the Diety,
But looking steadfast to the Deer,
To see if they were drawing near,
And at the last, without Remead,
He dang a Harts heels ov'r his head.
And sent him down to *Invercald*,
Or else at home a lie he tald.

By this time *Kerrow* was come home,
Where he got but a sad Welcome,
He got a charge for to compear
At *Castle-Blair* for *Athols* Deer;
Which News his Heart gave such a wound,
That instantly he fell a sound;
His Eyes turn'd as a sullid glass,
And like haw clay his hands and face,
His Feet as cold as any stone,
Thus he expir'd and gave a grone.

He did into this posture ly,
Till he was wakn'd with the Cry,
Which his Wife gave supposing Deed,
Her Husband was, alas she said,
How now lyes my husband here,
Dead for fear of *Athol's* Deer!

His Ears were pierced with her moan,
He looked up and gave a groan,

C

Then

Then he at her began to speer,
How long dead have I lyen here.
   To interrogat him *She* began,
Alas ! What have ye kill'd a Man ?
Or have ye seen an Apparition ?
That's put you in this sad condition ?
Or 'gainst Queen *Ann* committed Treason ?
Contrar to all Law and Reason ?
Tell me soon what ye have done ?
Against the Country or the Queen ?
Tell me, tell me in all haste,
My Patience cannot longer last,
Alas ! alas ! My heart is sad,
Tell me soon or I'll go mad.
   Alas I guilty am of Blood
Yet I am free of Homicide ;
I guilty am of Fish and Deer,
At *Castle-Blair* I must appear,
And afterward at *Aberdeen*,
O ! That Fish I had never seen ;
Duke *Athol* against me is inrag'd,
And many a Witness has he charg'd.
His Neighbour *Tom* upon the Morn,
Came home to gather in his Corn,
Which he left rotting with the weet,
And trampl'd under Cattels feet,
When all Men thought he had left Thrift,
And tean him to the Hills to shift.
   Now by this time the Dominie,
He thought the *Devil* was in *Glenshee*,
Because from fiends it had its name,
And how himself was us'd by them :
He thought, the *Devil* take you all,
Or Plagues of *Ægypt* on you fall,
He thought more than here's exprest,
Because he had no House to rest,   Then

Then he resolv'd to take him soon,
With all his speed to *Aberdeen*.
A Gentle-woman mov'd with shame,
How all the Countrey were to blame,
And how they idly spent the Summer,
And brought not home Bridge-trees nor Timber,
And yet remain'd as idle Drons,
She thought upon her little ones
Whom she lov'd as tenderly,
As the very Apple of her Eye.
    Then she thus to her Husband speak,
Ye know how all did promise break,
And now the Lade's to take's, farewell;
Because he's neither House nor School.
We'll build him one upon this side,
If he with us will grant to bide,
For he is one of the *Clanchatan*,
He'll be as true as steell or button,
I know before he break his word,
He'll choise to dy upon a Sword,
To this her husband did adhere,
For he was one who God did fear.
    Then she came east unto *Dalhinzean*,
And bids them bring their Trees to *Binzean*,
For we will build a School-house there,
Since they'll build none another where.
We will build one, on our own cost,
Before our Children all be lost,
Send ye down word to *Corridon*,
And all the People this side on
I pray you all do as I say,
And come away without delay.
The word went down to *Charles Small*,
He cry'd the Devill take you all,
Hast *Corridon* and *Dalhinzean*,
Haste, and bring your Trees to *Binzean*,

C 2

The

Then every one came with a Tool,
And Timber to rear up the School,
They wrought like mad, till Night did come,
When it was dark they all went home
They hastily again did meet,
And did put up their House compleat.
   The People on the other side,
Moved with Envy and with Pride,
Forth with they began to throng,
They'll do no right, they'll have no wrong,
They'll have the School on their own side,
Not for Profit, but for Pride.
Tom told the Master did not flatter,
He should not stay beyond the Water ;
Nor any other more than he,
That ever should be in *Glenshee*.
   Says *Rinavey*, I'll say not so,
For Heaven and Earth hath prov'd my Foe,
Since I did act against Ms. *John*,
I'll mould no more with the Church-men,
In that Affair I was so stout,
When all Subscriv'd, that I stood out;
I neither would hear Right nor Reason,
Although he had been cast in Prison :
I may with *Saul*, now justly cry,
Ms *John* more righteous is than I.
I've been a persecuting *Saul*,
O make me now a Praying *Paul*,
That I may no more have a hand,
'Gainst those who at the Altar stand,
A great Sigh and a Groan gave he,
And *Tom* began to pacifie.
   Neighbour *Tom*, I think ye're made,
To have such ire against the Lad,
For presently ye hear him say,
Where the first House is, there he'll stay,   If

If our's be first up on this side,
There he says, he shall abide,
If theirs be first beyond the Water,
There he'll stay, he does not flatter.
   Toms old and young with *Rinavey*,
Again appointed *Munenday*,
And at the *Cam's* about Day-light,
There meet this three Lairds of might,
Another Council there they held,
How they best a School might build ;
Says *Tom, Cams*, ye'll a couple be,
Two I and *Kerrow* this is three ;
Spittel the rest and *Rinavey*,
So they went forth and gave a Cry.
Come forth, come forth, ye Rustick Rable,
Come forth and build the Tower of Babel.
   Then to the Wood went all the Town,
For to cutt the tall Cedars down.
Each one with a Horse and Harrow
Trailing Timber to the *Kerrow*
Some had an Ax, and some a Wimble
But many more for haste came humle,
They had no Men to Couples ty,
On the Terrey they did cry,
A hog [hoy] for *Roy* come over the Water,
Come over and join us in this Matter,
Each one wrought as he'd been mad,
Building *Babel* as I said,
They knit their Couples not to Jaake
To never one they gave a balk ;
But did erect them to the Sky,
Till they should come on the next Day ;
But many of them did appear,
At *Athol's* Court for killing Deer,
Where some of them there did confess,
They trembling stood before his Grace,   And

And sweating too, their hearts did ake,
And Joints did like *Belshazzars* shake,
Which was enough to move the Pity,
Of Her who lives in *London* City.
The Prince of *Athol's* heart was soft,
And fill'd with Pity, when so oft
He saw him trembling almost dead,
And sweating each drop like a bead,
He past him till another time,
Though not absolved from the Crime,
He thinks his Grace of [at] this will nod,
He fears him more, than he fears God.
 By this the Building was delay'd,
After all their force was try'd,
As *Babels* Towr's fell to the ground ;
When God their Language did confound,
I think so hath he done to them,
For both their Works have prov'd the same ;
Their Couples by the wind did fall :
But yet again they say they shall,
Be once put up, and there shall be,
The Seminary of *Glenshee,*
And there they will bring Mr. *Smith,*
In spight of all his Friends and Pith,
When they do this (my Muse she shall,
If Ink be thick mix it with gall)
Contentedly with all my heart,
Then I shall pen a second part.

F I N I S.

Though

Though to my Muse it be disaster,
to answer such a Poetaster ;
Yet take these Lines when them you see
for scandalizing of Glenshee.

An answer to the *Black Smiths* sensless Poetry
anent the Building of the Schoolhouse of
Glenshee.

MY Muse is crost for to revise,
Lines which so highly I dispise,
Yet ere my Countrey be disgrac't,
Where Divine Providence me plac't,
I'll answer Mr. *Smith* the Fool,
Who in *Glenshee* doth keep the School,
As to his rhyme anent the building,
Of *Babell,* as he calls it scolding,
and make ingenuous Readers see,
that he amiss doth blame *Glenshee,*
Since this is slighted by the rest
Of Poets, I tho not the best,
Among us, yet will undertake ;
to make his Sophistry to quake.
    As to thy Preface it is Treason,
Both contrar to all Law and Reason,
thou fears not therein for to vent,
Reproach against the Government ;
as to thy Poetry its nonsense,
and therein not a word of bonsense
the first Line of these stupid verses
Is defective, and fit for a—s,
Most of the rest loves its example
more fit for Swine on them to trample,
than Men to read of understanding,
Who have their wills at their commanding.
                                              Thou

Thou says an hundred Merks we have,
Of Bishoprents our cost to save,
Because by drinking we are spenders,
By Whores and Dice ; no Money Lenders :
If we do this, thourt not behind us,
thy Vice and Luxury thou bind us,
to make the Christian World to know thee,
as we shall in thy Colours show thee.
　　Thou'll Drink, Carouse, both Swear and Curse,
and fiend a Peny in thy purse,
thy Whoredom doth right well appear,
although thou hast been short while here,
thy Love, nay, Lust drove thee right far
In time of Snow, even to *Braemar*,
to see thy Concubins and Dunties,
that thou might feel and f—k their C—t—s.
　　Thou tells one we resolv'd to Call,
Out of the Colledge *Marishall*,
One that hath Greek, and Latin speaks,
they are so large they may be dyks
If they be dyks, thou may be Morter
And do the office of the Porter
To keep the dyke from wind and weather,
Thou'rt made of Lime and sand, dirt rather,
thy Colledge has been at *Buckhaven*,
Where thou hast past thy time years seven
among the Salters and the Fishers,
Whom thou thy self calls thy wellwishers.
　　Though some of us Tobacco Smoak,
the reek doth never make us Choak,
either our Throats or stop our Nose,
as thy vile snichen, and thy brose
Which thou dost as thy God adore,
without which thou can live no more
than we can do without our breath,
take thou this Turd to pick thy Teeth.　　Thou

Thou calls us Fishers, and Deer killers,
browsters, Husbandmen, and Millers,
it is far better so to do,
than beg from door to door like you :
thy Giddy brain so full of boldness,
although thy Joints do shake for coldness,
that thou not only rails us all ;
but some by name thou dares to call ;
On *Tom* and *Kerrow* thou dost play
On *Finingand*, and *Rinavey*,
We'll answer at our names thou Ass,
and make thee from thy challenge pass.

    Thou says of *Tom*, he's quite all thrift,
And tane him to the hills to shift ;
It's like he would shift better there,
Than thou with all thy Clergy fair
Could do at *Rome*, or yet at *Naples*
Or Pastum fair, where grows good Aples :
But for evasion thou alledges,
his shifts not honest, but takes Pledges,
From *Athol's* Forrests or of *Marr*,
Or takes black fish with light of starr ;
Thou says he sent to *Invercall*,
Lest he among the *Grants* should fall ;
to *Invercall* he sent no Deer,
Of Captain *Grant* he had no fear,
Now where's thy lies and silly Rhyme ?
I fear thou'll perish for this Crime.

    Kerrow thou says and he were fishing,
and fill'd their breeks with dirt and pishing ;
thy words most nasty are and hateful,
and no less Calumning and Spitful :
They have more skill to keep their Breeks,
Than thou thy nose or yet thy Cheeks,
Polluted still with dirt and snuffing,
Or breath of Whores upon the puffing.

D   *Kerrow*

Kerrow thou says was made appear,
at *Atholls* Court for killing Deer,
the fear of which did strick him dead,
and filled both his heart and head
With fear to stand before his Grace,
With tears his eyes and all his face,
Thy Calumning will never end,
till God thee to thy grave do send,
It was not Pity but just Law,
That brought him out of *Atholls* paw.

　　Thou thought the Devil was in *Glenshee,*
because they were not kind to thee,
Indeed thy thoughts, have not deceived
thy self, for we have him received.

　　Thou Prays the Devil take us all,
Or Plagues of *Egypt* on us fall,
Before the Devil get one of us,
Or Plagues of *Egypt* seise us thus,
as thou dost pray he'll get thy self
With all thy vile and stinking Pelf
we mean thy Rhyme and not thy Gear
For Devil a farthing thou hast here.
Thou tells in triumph that thou hadst Friends
Although thou dwelt among the fiends,
to wit, of those who did abide,
Upon the Waters other side ;
that they took care to build a School,
Because the rest did play the Fool,
But know, and thereat be asham'd,
that this sad truth should once be nam'd
They did it not for thy deserving,
But were asham'd to see thee starving.

　　When word came down to *Charles Small,*
He cry'd the Devill take you all,
As thou dost say, but hold thy Tongue,
its not his ordinary Song.

We

We doubt not but ere long we'll find,
A Man agreeing to our mind,
who carefully will teach our Youth,
For thou hast such a burning Drouth,
that thou must run unto the Ale,
though School and Learning both should fail.
  Thou boldly brings in *Rinavay*,
In thy deriding scorn and play,
Confessing with a sigh and groan,
His evils done against Mes *John ;*
If he was guilty of offence,
It was his tender Conscience,
Made him reserv'd ere he did see,
Ms *John* by legal means made free ;
But now he loves him as his Heart,
'Gainst all his foes will take his part,
Exclame no more on *Rinavey*
He loves the Truth I may well say.
  Now *Smith* see if thou's got thy pay,
For stricking with thy Hammers ay,
Upon *Glenshee* since thou came here,
if not of that thou shalt be sure.
  Now Christian Brethren of *Glenshee*
take in good part what's done by me.
I have confuted Mr. *Smith,*
Your Adversar for all his pith,
If Ink be thick, he swears he shall,
To make it thin mix it with gall,
Contentedly with all his heart,
he says he'll Pen a second part.
We care not for his seed a fart,
Pen when he will his second part.

A Reply, or a Bow at Adventure (which drove the Author of the foregoing, from his lurking Holes) by R. S.

AN Answer to that Poetaster,
   Who serves the Devil who's his Master,
Who to vent his Prophanitie,
Thinks for to flatter our *Glenshee*,
By whom his Rhyme is much abhor'd,
Which he suppos'd would be ador'd.
   The Title breeds thee Shame and Lack,
Tho' thou designs me a *Smith* Black;
And says I've senseless Poetrie,
Anent the School-House of *Glenshee.*
   Fair Flowers have not the sweetest Smell,
As any Man of Sense can tell,
Yea *Lucifer* though he was fair,
From Heaven to Hell he did repair;
None (but a Brute) will make Reflection
Upon a reverend, grave Complection.
   My Name is from the King of Arts;
Which to the World more good imparts,
Yea ev'n to Kings, to Dukes and Earles,
Than Jasper Stones, or finest Pearles.
   Thou like a Basilisk would tear,
But yet must hide thyself for fear,
Such Hellish Imps sure never thrives,
They must run whom the Devil drives.
   Indeed if thou had right revis'd,
That which thy Brain-sick-head dispis'd,
Thou would have found thy self a Fool,
To speak of *Glenshee* or their School.
Thou art so far from being best
Of Poets, that they are disgrac'd,
                      Because

Because that Name thou dost pollute,
Thou silly stupid, senseless Brute,
Thou'rt guilty of Disgrace and Shame,
Because thou hast deny'd thy Name,
And consequently all thy Verses,
Which are too base for wiping A—s.

I'll let thee understand I know thee,
As by sure Tokens I shall show thee,
And prove thou art a greater Fool,
Than Mr. *Smith* that keeps the School.
I will thy Sophistry detect,
Before thy pow'r make mine to quake.

Which is not Sophistry, but Truth:
But now have at thee heartless Youth;
But I no more will write for thee,
Upon the People of *Glenshee*,
But some thing of the Truth I'll show,
To let the Reader better know,
That I am able to refute thee,
Although the Devil should recruit thee.

Thou says my Preface it is Treason,
Which shows thou'rt void of Sense and Reason,
Was it because in it was shown?
They did of late the King dethrone?
And idly set the Bishops by,
And in their Place fix'd Presbytry?
Or was't because I nam'd Tones?
Unto the Presbyterian Ones
Since each one has his Tone on Earth,
As proper to him as his Breath:
Thon senseless Sott thy self doth show
Thou art as ignorant's a Sow:
What sees thou here that's like to Treason,
But pardon Beasts for lack of Reason.

I'll pledge my Life, thou'll not dissent
From any present Government,   For

For very little Gain or Hire,
Thou'd bury Conscience in a Mire ;
For greed of Gain thou would not scorn,
For to subscrive the *Turks* Alcorn.
A present Life thou esteems more,
Than all Hopes of Eternal Glore.
Thou says the first Line of my Verses
Is defective, and fit for A—s ;
Thou art a Liar, all Poets ken,
The Defect's only in thy Brain :
And after they have wipt foul H—s,
They are too fine to cleanse thy Lips ;
And on the rest no Man can trample,
But Swine like thee, by thy Example,
Whom if they follow, they lack Reason,
But Beasts were never hang'd for Treason.

   Thou says, I'll drink, carouse, and curse,
And never a Penny in my Purse.
Thou do'st me square by thy own Rod,
And thinks because thou fears not God,
That every one is like to thee,
A cursed drunken Debauchee.
All who knows me, knows thou lies,
Such Godless Customs I dispise,
My Company is ay the best,
And Gentlemen who would detest,
All cursing drunken Debauchees,
Like thy Prophanity and Lies.
Of Money thou art an Adorer,
And yet of Drink thou'rt no Abhorer ;
'Tis known I gladly pay my shot,
If Gentlemen impede me not ;
Tho' thou delights such Lies to tell,
To make thy self an Heir of Hell.

   Indeed I rightly do remember :
I went to *Braemar* in *December;*   To

To see these generous Gentlemen,
Whose praise exceeds my Tongue and Pen,
To whom my Candor well appears,
That I disdain all Bauds and Whores,
But such base Acts are only thine,
The Draff is best belov'd of Swine;
Who hates all odoriferous Scents,
And glutts themselves with Excrements:
For Impudence it self would be
Ashamed to hear what's said by thee:
Neither my Honour or Good Name,
Can ever be stain'd by the same;
But bark on Curr, till thou grow hoarse,
My Fame is never a whit the worse.
 I'll prove it as my Verses speaks,
That Dominies they may be Dyks;
For in the *South* they are so large,
A Sutor got of thee the charge;
For to provide thee in a place,
(It seems indeed thou wanted Grace)
The Sutor made a publick Cry, }
At every house as he came by,
A Hoy who wants a Dominy.
It seem'd thou was a scurvie Futor,
Thou had no Patron but a Sutor,
Who had thee at command to fee,
On Earth thou'd no such Friend as he.
Tho' he'd not been thy Friend by blood,
Yet being a Beast he lov'd the brood.
 Again, to prove that they're not scant,
For when of late *Glenshee* did want;
Thou did petition by thy Letter,
And yet was never a whit the better;
And now thou thinks to take their Parts,
To see if that can melt their Hearts,
When I am gone for to receive thee,
But silly Fool, thy Thoughts deceive thee; For

For ay when thou speaks of *Glenshee*,
Then thou usurps the Pronoun *We*,
As thou art alwise an Intruder,
So each one here is thy derider.
    Thou Sot thou matter wants and stuff
To raill on me for taking Snuff,
A sinless Custom in repute,
Which none dispises but a Brute
That thou might raill with stinking words,
From Calder thou did borrow T—s,
Let Men of Judgement give thee praise,
To see thy Trophees buil't with these.
    As for the Colledge I was bred,
We were not both brought up indeed,
As by thy terms doth well appear,
The Devil himself would blush to hear,
What thy Tongue spitts out, O prophane !
To writ them would defile my Pen ;
To hear them spoke the Devill would hush
Alecto & Erinnys blush :
They greatly do defile the ear,
Of every one who doth them hear.
    If I did beg they were to blame,
They did me call before I came ;
Since they ought to've had that discretion,
To us'd me as became my station :
Which I did never effectively,
I thought it begging comp'ratively
To wit, that I should live so mean,
As me before no Man had seen.
But surely thou had taken't better,
Who was acquainted with the matter.
    But as to *Tom*, what I did say,
He knows it was in sport and play,
For he of knacks was never scant,
No Reason he a scorn should want ;   **Al**

Although thy foolish Rhyme alledges,
That he of *Athols* Deer took Pledges;
Which he did not (a Liar thou are,)
From *Athol* Duke or Earl of *Marr*,
But by his Masters own Command,
Of whom he holds both House and Land,
In's Forrest he a Deer caus'd fall,
And sent him down to *Invercall.*
For *Invercall* would not receipt,
A thing that's got by stealth or cheat.
His Candid Honour, it is clear,
That he regards no Pledge or Deer,
Of all the Forrests of *Braemar*,
Nor of the Prince that wears the Star,
For he doth live the World may see,
Under the Vine and sweet Fig-tree.
  It seems thou in my brain fears boldness,
As I into thy heart see coldness,
Since thou for fear can not abide me,
But must run to the Devil to hide thee.
Yet as a fool thou dost minace,
That I must from a challenge pass.
Though Cold had made my Joints to shake,
'Tis like my Pen will make thee quake,
Or else it'll make thy Courage heat thee,
To tell thy name, and then to beat me.
Thou thinks that I'm as fear'd as thou,
Who has less Courage than a Sow,
Thou both denys thy Name and Rhyms,
For fear thou Perish for such Crimes.
  And as again to *Kerrows* Cloaths,
Which thou compares unto my nose;
My Face and Nose all Persons see,
His Backside none saw that save thee,
Thou art the Sow who by thy Speeches,
Or with thy Tongue did cleanse his Breeches,

  E   And

And did them liberate from smell,
So for thy pains kiss thou his Tail.
Thou pleads his Cause, he'll thee permit;
But must find Caution not to bite.
What fill'd his Breeks I did not know,
Till thou who dighted them did show.
   I thought the Devill was in *Glenshee*,
As it on solid Grounds might be
With Holy *Job* he keeped tryst,
And *Josua* the Holy Priest,
As likewise in the Wilderness,
He tempted C. ev'n face to face,
Though he came here he found no rest,
Till he return'd back to thy Breast,
Thou offer'd here, they would not have thee,
And so for thee, they did receive me.
Thou see's thy Sophistry detected,
For all the art that thou objected;
Though Error be of ancient date
Yet by the Truth 'tis ay defeat.
   Fool thou objects I have no Pelf,
For greed of which thou'd hang thy self.
No marvel though sometimes I'm scant,
The freest hearts oftimes doth want,
For thirty pieces, yea for less,
Thou wou'd run cursed *Judas* Race;
But since thy will it is so good,
It'll be accepted for the deed.
   I'll tell't again that I have Friends,
And hated am by none but Fiends,
And who the Truth cannot abide,
But still at it will carp and chide,
And doth it ay calumniat,
With Eagerness, Envy, and Hate,
My Friends they daily do increase,
But thine on Earth turns less and less,

I know not what they are in Hell,
Where thou I fear ere long must dwell,
When thou goes there thou best can tell. }

My House was built for my deserving,
I never was redact to starving,
Poor fool 'tis thy simplicitie,
To think each one has been like thee.

And as again to *Finingand*,
I did but work at his Command.
For he is just like *Herostratus*,
To raise his Fame he will be *gratus*.

And what thou says of *Rinavey*,
I wish it were as thou dost say,
He's turn'd his Friend against his will,
Because he could not do him ill;
Just like a Thief that must turn leel,
Because he has not strength to steal,
Or like a Dog that will not bite;
Because his Teeth has fail'd him quite.

Thou Map of all Disgrace and Shame;
Who basely has deny'd thy Name;
Before thy flesh were stigmatiz'd,
Thou would deny thou was Baptiz'd,

What Honour can thou get or wish,
To shoot at me out of a Bush?
A thing below all generous Spirits,
But best becomes all Hypocrites.
But yet thy Balls they have no force,
Their smoak may only stink thy Nose,
As their sound doth defile the Ear,
Of every one who doth them hear.

Thou says I have a burning Drouth,
Now, herein if thyself speak Truth;
Though I should drink, my sin is less
Than thine, who drinks unto excess,

F 2
And

And yet has neither Drouth nor Cause,
Thou both breaks G—s and natures Laws.
    Poor fool thought thou to kill me dead,
And yet so fear'd was for my fead,
That like a Thief thou ran away,
And then cry'd thou, gave *Smith* his pay?
    I need no Hammers to withstand thee,
Since all do see my Pen commands thee,
Thou threats that *Smith* by the's be paid,
I pray thee do as thou hast said,
For I expect but easy blows,
From th' Cowards who stoutest words ay shows,
Tell me thy Name, show me thy Face,
Or hold thy peace to thy Disgrace.

Robert Smith.

By the fore Lines, the Hypocrite was forc'd to un-
    vail himself.   Thus he begins.

IS *Smith* again begun to blow,
    Out stinking Wind from Bellows slow,
And do his Hammers strike with might,
Or doth he with a nail string fight;
I thought he had been gone ere now,
That he of Hell might get a view,
To see *Vulcanus* his grim chief,
And *Pluto* that black ugly Thief;
his kind Companions who him sends,
some fire-brands which he out sends,
against those whom they cannot harm,
since they come from so weak an arm;
because that now *Glenshee* hath beat thee,
and every honest Man doth hate thee,
thou with thy Hammers stricks at me,
which I regard less than a flee,

Thou

Thou tells my name in Terms full plain,
which to my Candor is no stain,
A *Jasper* stone which thou dost scorn,
The heavenly Buildings do adorn,
And is first of the Twelve Foundations,
In new *Jerusalems* Situations:
No marvel thou do mock that place,
Where Saints behold God's blessed Face,
because therein thou hast no right,
Of it thou'll never get a sight.
but wilt be thrown into the fire
blown by the bellows of God's ire
As thou art nam'd from *Vulcans* Art,
So thou with him will get thy part,
and drink his nectar in Hells Closet,
ev'n melted brim-ston pitch and roset.

It's brain sick heads just like thine own,
Says Lucifer from Heaven came down,
For Lucifer in Heaven is still,
as is confirm'd by Men of skill,
that bright and lucid Morning Star
Whose light exceedeth very far,
All other Stars, it doth display,
and Ushers in the lightsome day,
But no marvell though here he err,
beasts no conclusion can inferr,
and all the World may clearly see,
Smiths never knew Astronomie.

In vindicating your *Glenshee*,
I always us'd the Pronoun *We*,
good reason for they did intreat,
my help in their name thee to beat.

Thou says that Poets are disgrac't,
because my name among them's plac't,
I am ashamed of the Name,
Because thou arrogats the same   Which

Which thou deserves as well as Swine
are worth to drink Canary Wine,
Or *Denmarks* Dog for to be King,
Or Dumbies getting praise to sing,
Or Oxen for to eat with Princes,
Or thy lies to be call'd Defences,
Or base Pretenders for to Reign
Or Strangers Bastards to be King,
Or Drunkards to be call'd good Fellows
Or Gluttons to get greater Bellies.
Or Poison to be call'd good Food,
Or Sin it self call'd Moral Good.
   I never did deny my Name,
Of it I need to think no shame,
more precious in Earth and Heaven,
than all that ever by *Smiths* were given,
I did it not proclaim, because,
an Advocat in Civil Laws,
his Clients Name, and not his own
doth arrogat, as is well known,
but now when thou dost mention me,
and like a Coward flees from *Glenshee*,
I'll tell my Name to thy Disgrace,
and likewise let thee see my face;
as thou didst soon flee from *Glenshee*,
I hear so wilt thou do from me,
and take thee to thy Ancient Trade
wherewith thou from thy youth wast bred
Which some say was by stealing Sheep,
Some say thy Brothers thou did keep,
I mean the vile and nasty Swine,
whose Noses are more clean than thine.
   If I did thee accuse of Treason,
I'll make it plain to human Reason,
that thou art guilty, for thou Clown,
thou blames the taking off the Crown,   From

From *Popish James*, that Tyrant grand,
who would have over-thrown our Land,
had not his Power been soon cut down,
And Royal *William* got the Crown.
Thou dost bewail the Mitred Priests,
Calamities, within whose Breasts
is Vipers Poison to infect
God's Holy People and Elect,
They were but always idle drons,
While they had power to sound their tons
like Oxen fatted in the stall,
not fit for any work at all,
and contrar to God's Ordination,
Usurping stiles above their station,
taking on them Supremitie,
where God commands Equalitie,
Art thou not guilty then of Treason,
but Beasts have not the use of Reason
else thou would hang for this thy Crime,
Which thou hast publish't thus in rhyme.
    Thou says for Money I'll not scorn
for to subscribe the *Turks* Alcorn
I truly think thou Devils Minion,
thou'rt one of *Mahomets* Opinion,
that is far better Faith for thee,
than any ways it is for me,
For this thy Faith thee well assures
Thou'll get Ten Virgins to be Whores,
Whom every day thou mayest know,
Yet Virgins still if it be so.
This greater pleasure in thee raises,
Than singing God's Eternal Praises
With Hallelujahs at his Throne,
From whence all Whores must be gone.
    Thou says I greatly am to blame,
For giving things their proper Name,   thou

thou Fool, I knew thy thick-sculd head
My meaning had not understood,
If I had us'd Heroick Dictions,
thou would have thought they had been fictions;
the Lyrick Poet *Horace* says,
C—ts were the cause of Wars and Pleas
such Instances enough I know,
Though to a Brute I'll not them show.
    A Sutor of me ne're had Power,
As *Satan* hath of thee each Hour,
He only told where I did dwell,
So much I never bad him tell;
but silly sot thou'rt void of sense,
and vents thy stupid Ignorance
Christ who was Gods beloved Son,
was shown to Men by Baptiz't *John*
his Gospel preach't was to the Poor,
In means as well as Spirit I'm sure,
being but silly Fisher Men,
as Holy Scripture lets us ken,
I never did beg of *Glenshee*
that I might be their Dominie.
    Yea I had a far better place,
And has this day (by God's good grace.)
I borrowed T—ds indeed from *Calder*,
for to besmear this stinking scalder,
Because I use not stinking T—ds
I'll pay him with much fairer words.
    Does thou yet speak of Education,
of School or Colledge in this Nation?
thou hast no Latine, Greek or Logick,
nor any Art, but may be Magick.
I heard thou wast at *Aberdeen*,
dighting somes and others Sheen,
that is the skill thou brought from thence,
but thou must get thee gone from hence.   Thou

Thou says I'll not take ill to beg,
as being wont before to thig,
but thou'rt a Liar it is well known,
I always liv'd upon my own:
Yea there is some in this Countrie,
do know my honest Pedegree,
Tho thou to get a livelyhood,
thought dighting Shoes an office good.
When *Invercald* thee did refuse
to keep his gate, who can thee chuse?
thou by thy vain and silly jests,
intrudes thy self to others Feasts,
I'll not deny that I'm Baptiz'd,
although I should be Atomniz'd:
But thou'd deny that thour't Baptiz'd,
and let thy self be Circumcis'd,
Were it not it would hurt thy P—k,
no other thing would make thee stick.
I think I've done as I did say,
And given the Black-Smith his pay.
    Though you come with your Pen and Hammers
And join your Tongue which always Stammers.
My Pen alone it will withstand thee,
and is too able to command thee,
Fall to thy Books, and fix thy study,
for thou'll hing shortly in the Widdy.
thou crys to know my Name and Face,
I'll show these both to thy Disgrace,
I'll now silence thy shouts and hallows,
Look to my Name; for here it follows.

Jasper Craig.

Mr. Robert Smith's *Answer to the forgoing Lines,*
Thus begins.

A Return to that *Jasper stone,*
Who is the Devils Paragon;

F   His

His chiefest agent here on Earth,
Exceeding all the Shire of *Perth*,
In Swearing, Drinking, and Prophaneness;
Unthankfulness, Pride, and Uncleanness;
In Lying, Greed and Monstrous folly,
Railing at Sacred thing and Holy.
As I shall prove (before I part)
By Witnesses; not Poets Art,
Such Witnesses as will not Lye,
Nor can deny what I'm to say.

    A Black-Smiths Bellows or his Hips,
Blows sweeter than thy Nose or Lips.
Which stinking are and still doth smell,
Of Dirt since thou cleans'd *Kerrows* Tail:
Black colour it would be disgrac'd
Upon thy face for to be plac'd,
And so would red, or Colour white,
Though Brimston Smoak has tane delight,
To show its Colour, it thee paints,
And makes thy Hue like Excrements.
That neither Honest Lass nor Whores,
Can fancy thee for *Venus* Powers.

    Unworthy Brute I am not gone.
To see what is by right thy own,
Thou best deserves old *Vulcans* fire,
To purge away the base desire,
Which thy Tongue shows is in thy heart,
With *Pluto* thou deserves to smart.

    Thou base vile Excrement of Earth,
Defiling air with stinking breath,
My Pen has made thee to confess
And tell thy Name to thy disgrace.

    Which thou says is a *Jasper* stone,
Laid first in Heavens foundation,
The goodly stones that are above,
Are fixt and never will remove,   Each

Each *Jasper* there is holy sure,
But thou'rt on Earth, and most impure,
Thou'rt fitter for another thing,
To be set in the Devils Ring.
If thou be haughty of thy Name,
Why, but the Devil may be the same ?
Since he is call'd God of this World,
As thou'rt call'd *Jasper* in *Straharld;*
Although that Name was put on thee,
A *Craig* that could not beautifie,
Because in thee there's nothing precious,
Thy name can never make thee gracious.
   In nature thou'rt as mad's a stag,
Thy Surname suits thee better *Craig,*
On which the Serpents loves to trade,
They're in thee hatcht, they're on thee bred,
On *Craigs* they alwise love to be,
The old one he possesses thee.
Thou shows their Venom's in thy heart,
Thy tongue it spits on all a part ;
Reviling Kings, and Bishops Holy,
Loving by this to show thy folly,
Thou guilty art of Blasphemy,
In all thy unclean Poetry ;
How dares thou ev'r Religion stain,
To write or take His Name in vain ?
Thou Rash, thou beastly fool, pray, stand,
Reflect upon the Third Command,
Poor Wretch ; I bid thee dread and fear,
And from such Blasphemy forbear.
Whose ears would not (save *Atheists*) tingle ?
To hear how thou thy nonsense mingle ?
Some Pious words, and some Prophane,
Some time to Heaven, and then again,
Thou dips thee down again in Stygian,
Railing at Kings, and all Religion.

Ther's

There's none of sense or wit can praise thee,
As for thy Pen it'le never raise thee,
Thy empty scull and thy dull brains,
Makes thee to beg from others Pens.
Thou art so scarce of Rhyme and words,
I made thee to confess with T—s,
Which thou did borrow from another.
Thou borrows here two Lines together,
To wit, the Brimstone Pitch and Roset,
Which thou drank last into Hells Closet.
To *Lucifer* thou's such a Love,
Thou takes his part, thinking to prove,
That he in Heaven doth remain,
But silly fool thy thoughts are vain :
From that name he has, thou declines,
And flys to the Cœlestial signs,
Thinking with thy mad Sophistry,
To keep the Devill still on high.
All knows (save Brutes) while he in Heaven
Was, to him that pure Name was given,
And proper is to each Star bright,
To call them all bringers of Light,
But thou knows no Equivocations,
Nor yet Grammatical Expressions,
For thou may just so in this manner
Call *Fish* a Star, when drest for Dinner ;
Or *Dog*, or *Boar*, when dead a Starr ;
Or *Sheep*, or *Rame*, Weapons of War ;
When on their back grows purest Wool,
Where's thy Astronomy ? Blind Fool ;
By this the World may know and see,
That *Smith* may know Astronomie,
To which *Craigs* can have no pretence,
They being Creatures void of sense.
Though in thy head thou hast a Bee,
And thought to vindicat *Glenshee*.   Each

Each one of them they were asham'd,
To hear the horrid Lyes thou nam'd,
Their vindication it was such,
As sunk them deeper in the Ditch;
Because thou Ly'd and played such pranks,
Thou's got the Devil to thy thanks.

Thou nasty Sow, thou silly rat,
Thou calls thy self their Advocat,
But thou can never plead their cause,
A Beast was never skill'd in Laws.
All who consider right must say,
Thy self fled from *Glenshee* not I,
Nothing will make me from thee flee,
But thy most horrid Blasphemie,
Or else thy lies or words prophane,
Which doth defile the ears of Men.

For me I would not guilty be,
To write so base prophanitie,
Neither would any who has Grace,
No not to please all *Adam's* race.
For thy defence thou makes Citations,
Of Heathens, who had such Expressions,
No Heathen ever yet did use,
The vile Expressions thou dost chuse;
No Man with such did paper blot,
Rochester and thou base sot,
But what is most into the heart,
The tongue must indicat a part,
But Swine they alwise love dung Hills,
Of Excrements they'll eat their fills.

In Labouring to fix on me Treason,
Thou's quite exhaust thy sense and Reason,
And hast thy self involved in,
A Labyrynth of shame and sin.

Thou base thou brutish beastly thing,
The World he knows he was a King,   Come

Come of the Royal Blood and Race,
This all the World must confess ;
Likewise he got the Crown and Throne,
And why not since they were his own.
His Royal Offspring *Ann* this Day,
Her Fathers Scepter yet doth sway ;
Long may she live to do the same,
That all the World may hear her Fame.
Than me thou ought to hang far rather,
For railing on her Royal Father,
Whom all Men knows they did dethrone ;
And took from him what was his own :
Though *Saul* he sinn'd in *Israel*,
And from the Throne deserv'd to fall,
Yea, though he *David* did abuse,
(After Jehovah did him chuse)
Yet *David* did him not revile,
But gave him still his proper Stile,
As thou base Excrement of Earth,
Revils a King with stinking breath ;
Thy due Reward is a Dogs dead,
For revileing a crowned Head.
   Its Vipers Poyson in thy Breast,
Makes thee revile both King and Priest,
How dares thou (base unworthy Swine)
Speak once of Kings, or Men divine ?
Or blame the Sacred Ordinations ?
Of those ordain'd to Rule the Nations ?
Here thou dost act the *Devil's* Part,
And shows what's most into thy Heart.
Thou base unworthy scurvie Futor,
Thou art below a nasty Sutor,
Who did of late thee Patronize,
Who is't that thou can equalize ?
Thou art below all *Adam's* Race
Thou Mass of Shame, thou Stain of Place.

                         Thou

Thou art the Extract of all Evills
Spewing Venome, like the *Devil's.*
   I'le prove (for gain) thou would not scorn,
For to subscribe the *Turks Alcorn ;*
Thou base, thou greedy beastly Clown,
Thou left *Dalrullian* for a Crown,
Who show'd thee kindness in thy need,
When thou'd most starv'd for want of food,
When thou was fill'd, thy Heart so raise,
Thou made *Acrostick* to his Praise,
As *Alan'quich* can testifie,
And prove the Truth what here I say.
When he thy head set up the water,
On him thou did both ly and clatter,
As I did hear thee sensless Mouse,
Do in *McWillie's,* where *Whitehouse*
Did take his part, and thee silence,
And make thee pass from thy nonsense:
Glenkillry he can this declare,
For he was present likewise there.
   Thou shows thou hast less gratitude,
Than Beasts of the most savage brood,
If any Dog his Bread had got,
As long as thou did (Graceless Sot)
From *Dalrullian* he would show,
A greater gratitude than thou ;
The Dog would him defend from foes,
But thou him rails where e're thou goes:
Go learn thou of some savage Brute,
To lead thy Life far more discreet ;
King *Alexanders* famous Horse,
May in thy Conscience breed Remorse,
So may the Elephant of *Porus,*
Who serv'd their Masters in their Sorrows:
For railing thou deserves the Halter,
He was the first who gave thee Shelter,   Thy

Thy Railing may thy self disgrace,
But never can his Praise make less,
This will be honest *Bleatouns* Thanks,
When thou leaves him, thou'le play such Pranks:
Thou dost his honest house prophane,
And's like to bring on it a stain.
   I'le prove thou art a base Blasphamer,
A Liar, a Drunkard, and Defamer;
For Proof of this the East Barron
Of East *Straloch* and *Tullacarran*,
Honest *Dounie Dirnenyen*,
And all the rest good Gentlemen,
John Robertson, and *Charles Small*,
Who took thee up, when thou did fall,
Just like a Sow among the Dub,
And then swear thou would pay thy Club,
Likewise Clerk *Millar* in *Dunkell*,
And he who to them fill'd the Ale,
Yea all of them did see thee drunk,
And heard thee swear which might thee sunk:
Thou swear by G. twice openly,
Thou was not drunk as all did say;
How dares thou with thy brazen face,
Deny that thou did not transgress?
Which I have prov'd thou silly Brute,
By Gentlemen of good Repute,
None of them will, nor can deny:
What I've said here in Poetry:
   Yea thou was husht out to the door,
When thou (like Hell) began to roar,
If Judges suffer this to pass,
Each Country Clown may them minace.
   Again on Saturday before,
Thou likewise was put to the door,
For Swearing, Curseing, Drunkenness:
The Witnesses for proof of this   Is

Is Mr. *Robert Robertson,*
And all that were that place upon,
Glenkillry, *Whitehouse* can declare,
What I've said here, and meikle mair.
Who doubts the truth of this may speer,
No Gentleman will be a Liar.
    As what thou says upon my Name,
Get any who can prove the same,
In all *Strahardle*, or *Glenshee*,
Or yet upon the Water of *Dee*,
Where most part of the Gentlemen,
Of both the Countries do me ken :
I say, show one who can declare,
They saw me drunk, or heard me swear,
Or yet defile my Tongue or Pen,
Or other Ears, speaking prophane ;
As thou dost still thou beastly Knave,
Both swear, and curse, yea drink and rave,
In Terms obscene, with Tongue and Pen,
To please the *Devil*, or get Gain.
Thou *Devil's* Limb who dare once peep,
And say for's, Life, that I steal'd Sheep,
None for their Necks, it dares to say,
Else they by Law like Dogs should dy :
If thou would tell me so in Prose,
I'll take my hand from off thy Nose,
In spight of all that'le take thy part,
I'd make thee for the same to smart.
    Invercald he laughs to hear
Thy Nonsense, silly common Liar,
Because thou sayes he me refus'd,
I'm sure for's gate he'd not me chus'd.
    Yea when I was at *Aberdeen*,
I'd better for to dight my Sheen
Than thou, or he that patroniz'd thee,
And cry'd till he got one who chus'd thee :

G

But

But Sutors brats speaks ay of sheen,
And unclean tyks of things unclean,
For this I witness thy foul speeches,
Thou us'd in cleansing *Kerrows* Breeches.
    If thy sight were as goods thy smell,
Which the attract to *Kerrow's* tail,
Thy reeling eyen had surely seen,
My Face and Nose that both were clean,
Thy squaint looks makes thee miss the mark,
The Swine sees best into the dark.
    Thou sayes I by my silly Jests,
Intrudes my self to others Feasts,
I am not guilty of Intrusion,
For which thou gets oftimes Extrusion,
And must begone like any Beast,
For Blasphemy and not for Jest.
    I can jest with good Company,
And from offending keep me free,
But thou'rt a Beast void of all reason,
If not base dog shou'd hang'd for Treason,
For thy prophaning sacred things
As holy Bishops and great Kings.
    As for Religion thou hast none,
Thy Bible's sure the Alcoran:
The holy Bishops thou miscalls,
And calls them Oxen fed in stalls;
Thou'rt not a Presbyterian,
The World knows they're not prophane,
Neither Drunkards, nor Blasphemers;
No Quaker, for they're not Defamers;
No Papist, for thou keeps not Lent;
No Christian, thou dost not Repent;
The World knows thou'rt not a Jew,
Thou'll eat the flesh of Pig or Sow,
Thou'rt Atheist, or Infidel,
Or shame a thing that Man can tell.   Thou

Thou sayes there's some in this Country,
That knows thy hateful Pedegree,
Which if they do, they surely know,
The Dregs of all Men here below,
Show Man or Woman of Repute,
Who can commend them silly Brute.
They are so base that thou denys them!
And why but others should dispise them?
But what they are, and how they fare,
I know not well, and less I care,
So here with them I'll end compleat,
The Trees are ill, but worse the Fruit.

As to thy Poetry and Railing,
I pray thee for to mend thy spelling,
Into appear write thou two pp's,
Likewise to add put thou two dd's,
Office of two ff's is the better,
Begin each Line with a big Letter.
So should thou do each proper name,
But thou to Poets art a stain,
Parenthesis, is most unfit,
To end a Paragraph with it.

I'll prove Defects, and odd Redundance,
And nonsense in thy Lines aboundance,
These things would Poets all disgrace,
Among their Names thy Name to place,
Thou ought to be whipt with the Taws,
Because thou breaks the Grammer Laws,
Dare thou again with open face,
Except it be to thy Disgrace,
Usurp or take a Poets Name,
Thy Ignorance disgrace the same.

Thou dregs of shame, and all disgrace,
Thou scorn of time, thou stain of place,
Who are sunk down to that degree,
Below the reach of Infamie.   Thou'rt

G 2

Thou'rt Excrement of all the Creation,
For this, thy tongue and pen's probation,
Now when I've done, I've prov'd no more,
Than all who knew thee knew before,
To write more, might import as much,
As some believ'd thou were not such.
   Fall on again with all thy pith,
Try what thou'll gain from

                      Robert Smith.

The Answer to the foregoing Lines. Thus begins.

THE Witnesses whom thou dost name,
   I know They're Men of Note and Fame :
Yet none of them will say of me,
What is most basely said by thee.
   If I did swear it was a Truth,
Which then proceeded from my Mouth,
To wit that then I was not drunk,
(Though thou with Ale was almost sunk)
To swear the truth is not a stain,
Nor taking God's bless'd Name in vain,
If done with reverence as by me,
Who fears His Holy Majestie.
   Thou mockest at my Christian Name,
Why ? It's because thou'rt void of shame,
And of the fear of God and Grace,
When thou reviles my Name or Face.
   Though I a *Jasper* be on Earth,
Residing in the shire of *Perth*,
Thy purpose yet thou dost not gain,
for thou all *Jaspers* dost disdain,
and sets before them *Vulcans* Art,
Who's ever in thy Mouth and Heart,
A Craig is a most sure Foundation,
To build on it Fortification,   For

For this which I may tell in Meeter,
Christ surnam'd his Apostle *Peter*,
Which signifies a Rock or Craig,
Rail then thy fill thou old blind Nagge ;
None ere writ such stupiditie,
As in thy Lines is said by thee.

No accident can be disgrac't,
On what e're Subject it be plac't,
It hath it's being in another,
It's without Substance *Nonens* Brother.

Thou likewise argues brutishlie,
think to make it Sophistrie,
That whereby I did clearly prove,
That *Lucifer* is still above,
Thou says the Devil got that name,
but pray tell who gave him the same,
If any, sure its but a Brute,
tell me his name I'll him confute,
Thou sees I to thy self apeal,
and yet thou constantly dost fail,
Thou never will wipe of the stain,
A word thou canst not say again,
Thou canst not answer to the matter,
But still dost rail and nothing better.

Thou says I borrowed here two lines,
Which shows no wit within thee shines,
Thou blinded wretch whom all abhorr,
Where saw thou e're these lines before,
But hold thy peace and lick the T—ds.
I can give *Calder* better words.

Thou hellish wretch whom all disdain,
How dares thou say I speak profane ?
What as profane thou didst abhorr,
I vindicated here before,
Yet thou rejects my clear probations,
Because of *Horace* I've Citations,   *Paul*

Paul Epimenides doth cite,
to prove the vitiousness of *Crete,*
Even Heathens though they us'd such dictious
Were very far from thy base Actions,
Yea Christians do use,
As I can show thee if I please,
Montgomerie, Polwart, Men of note,
Have words as ill by every jot;
And so hath likewise *Samuel Colvill,*
the Son of Lady *Lizbeth Melvill.*
Does thou yet vindicat King *James,*
Whom every honest Man still blames;
I know he was a King by Birth,
Not sure by merit or by worth,   .
who e're they were did him Dethrone,
the fault was surely all his own,
His Tyranny the World doth know,
was worse than *Sauls* this I could show,
But since he's dead I'll let him ly,
Run to his grave in haste and cry,
That I against him did speak Treason,
yet on my side did still keep reason:
Likewise the just Laws of the Land,
Contemned by this fire-brand.
Thou sayest like a witless scullian,
That I'm ungrateful to *Dalrilyon,*
Whatever I said of his name,
I'm not ashamed of the same.

    I made a Crostick to his Praise,
I understood not then his wayes,
My words agreed to my thought,
When otherways I saw he wrought,
I told but how he used me,
But rail'd not as thou, on *Glenshee.*

    What holy Bishops does thou mean,
Is that the Priest of *Aberdeen?*   It

It seems he was not very holy,
A Whore provocked him to folly,
to wit, the Lady of *P——r*,
Who drew him in to a deep fur,
Or rather into a deep ditch.

    Or ist't that Bishop of *Dunkell?*
Of whom our Historys do tell,
That he blest God he never knew,
The Old Testament, or the New?
Or is it *S—p* that Reverend Father?
Who chused a good Stipend rather,
Than to be true unto his trust,
To God and Man he was unjust;
The *Scottish* Church he did betray,
And strove to ruine it alway.

    Or is he *P——n* by name?
Who suffered Reproach and shame,
He to a Lady gave a Ring,
And with a Clout that wipt her Thing,
He upon Sunday dight his mouth:
All persons know I speak the truth.

    Or is it that the Ordination,
Is of it self a holy Station?
Although prophanest Men do use it,
Why then do Holy Men refuse it?
I'll hold thou'll not find *Dioikesis*
Nor Hierarchick *Kibernesis*
In the New-Testament Dispensation,
They were but Types from the Creation,
Till Christ the Gospol did display,
When he's come should wear away.

    Thou never can clear thy self of Treason,
for thou'rt so void of Sense and Reason,
That even though thy Cause were just,
Thou could not plead it witless beast.

                    What

What hath thy stinking Nose been smelling,
When thou reproves me for my spelling,
for every one that's wrong in mine,
I'm sure there's more than six in thine.
   Where are these defects and redundance,
Of which thou says there are abundance
Into my Lines I pray thee show them,
That I my self may likewise know them;
Show in my Lines a word of nonsense,
Or in thine own a word of bonsense,
I boldly challenge thee to do it,
Neglect not, since I put thee to it,
I'll yet assume a Poet's Name,
To do which thou should think great shame,
My little finger, or a lith
of it, will conquer silly *Smith*,
Go take thy Hammers shoe thy Nagge,
for thou'll not pick at

                       Jasper Craig.

Mr. Smith's *Answer to* Mr. *Craig.*

NOw *Craig* think shame of all thy Actions,
   Thy shameful Swearing and Distractions,
Thy Drunkenness and thy Prophanness
And all thy Dictions of Uncleanness;
I'll prove it plainly in thy face,
And tell thee of thy own disgrace.
   Was thou not drunk I thee enquire?
When I brought thee through many a Mire;
Yea many a time I'm sure thou fell,
And made the obesance unto Hell.
Ask thou thy Master (graceless sot)
Whether thou was Drunk or not?
When he dang thee by Argument,
Till thou began nonsense to vent.

                              For

For which thou did Appologize,
Upon the morn, and beg'd excuse
These generous Gentlemen can show,
That thou was drunk like any Sow,
For which (as I said heretofore)
They did extrude thee to the Door,
With great Blasphemy in thy Mouth,
In Swearing to a great non-truth,
Thou swear by G. thrice (all did hear)
Thou was not drunk with Ale or Beer,
If thou was not what needed thou,
To Swear and Curse thou was not fow ?
The world knowes that never an Oath,
Was needful to a known truth.
Yea when a Matter is in doubt,
With reverence it is gone about,
None ought to swear till call'd by Law,
Which thou was not as all Men saw.
　　To swear the truth, if't be no stain,
Nor taking His bless'd Name in vain,
If this be true: by what thou says,
The Saints in Heaven may swear alwise,
For surely every word is truth ;
That doth proceed out of their Mouth,
This Doctrine sure is of the Devil,
To ruine Souls in sin and evil.
　　Although the Matter had been true,
As it was not thou Drunken Sow ;
One Oath to vindicat is right,
But thou swear thrice against the Light,
As every Witness can attest,
Although that Death were at their breast.
But whoso will may at them speer,
And then thou'll know who is the Liar.
　　Thou says I mock thy Christian Name,
No Christian ever had the same,

　　　　　　H　　　　　　　　　Thou

Thou said the *Jasper* I did scorn,
The Heavenly Buildings did adorn.
And now thou says thou'rt upon Earth,
Residing in the Shire of *Perth*,
Consider now thy Logick fictions,
Are they not obvious Contradictions!
Unless that *Jasper* was the Throne,
Which *Beelzebub* did sit upon,
It seems when he came down to Hell,
That *Jasper stone* it with him fell;
For otherwayes it could not be,
In Shire of *Perth* and Heaven too.
   Yea that which thou calls *Vulcans* Art,
(As said before) it doth impart
More good to all who draweth Breath,
Than all the *Jasper Craigs* on Earth,
By it all Mankind have their Bread,
Therefore it is the King of Trade.
Thy Tongue thy own Name loudly crys,
And sets thy self above the Skys;
But instantly thou falls to Earth,
And now Lurks in the Shire of *Perth*.
By Name and Surname thou'rt a Stone,
Most fit for Satan's Ring and Throne;
A Craig, indeed a firm Foundation,
Fit for the Devils habitation.
   An accident may be disgrac'd,
If not upon fit Subjects plac'd.
Yea Beauty surely would be stain'd,
Sound doctrine it would be prophan'd,
If thou of them had any part,
Because the Devil has thy heart.
   Yea *Nonens* it a being had,
Ev'n long before the World was made,
All Created Beings had their rise,
From faultless *Nonens* non denys;   *No-*

Nonens at first by God's Command,
Turn'd Heaven and Earth, yea Sea and Land,
And by his great word fill'd the Creation,
And yet took nothing from its station,
Speak thou no more of spotless *Nonens*,
For all thy Arguments are nonsense.

    I'll unto *Kirkwood* thee refer,
He calls the Devil *Lucifer*,
So doth a hunder Thousand more,
Who wit and Learning have in store)
Look to his vocables thou'll see,
It bright and obvious to thy Eye,
Now hold thy peace and become mute,
I've prov'd thee in this Point a Brute.

    Now here I'll prove thou inserted
(Of the Womans universe inverted)
Two Lines ; because of thy dull Brains
Thou'rt forc't to beg from others strains.

    Thou monstrous Map of all Uncleanness,
To vindicat thy base Prophanness,
How dares thou cite the blest St. *Paul?*
Even to the danger of thy Saul,
Show thy Expressions graceless sot)
In all the Books that these Men wrote ;
Thy'd rather chuse to die on Swords,
Than write or speak such prophane words,
But thou by Lies would hide Transgression,
And go to Hell without Confession.

    Hold thou thy Tongue, base hellish tyke,
Keep silence dog, and no more speak
Of that brave Royal King, he's gone,
From Earth to Heaven to a Throne,
Which Men nor Devils never can shake,
Nor yet his Crown nor Scepter take :
Thou says that thou (base Brute) could show,
His Tyranny while here below,   For

For to be worse than *Saul's* ; but Brute,
Tell out his Crimes, I'll thee confute,
But let the Dog bark at the Roe ;
And Sutors bratts at Kings also,
The Raven hates the pleasant Dove,
A Dog to Lambs had never Love,
Thou ought to cleanse thy stinking Mouth,
Yea even to speak of him the truth :
Thou art both void of sense and Reason,
Or else base Dog thou'd hang'd for Treason.
   The Bishop of Old *Aberdeen*,
The Pious Life he lives is seen,
He Preaches every Sabbath-Day,
Although his Rents be tane away,
His Lady thou base dog calls Whore,
The World knows that thou'rt a Liar,
No Man can Whoredom on her prove,
And why but good Men might her love ?
Though it had been as thou dost say,
Yea *Peter* did his L. deny,
No Man did it object to him,
But thou of *Satan* art a Limb ;
For to show evils and hid good,
Thou'rt sure a Whelp of *Satans* brood.
   As to the Bishop of *Dunkell*,
He might have said, (thy self some tell)
To wit, in's Life he never knew,
The Old Testament or the New ;
And yet been as knowing a Man,
As is this day below Queen *ANN*.
The Scriptures they are so profound,
That few on Earth can reach their Ground,
Now each beheaded fool's so vain,
And thinks he can them all explain,
At no mysterious Points they'll stick,
Yet will each other Contradict.   And

And as again to Bishop *Sharp*,
For him no Bishop thou can carp,
He was but a false Puritan,
And turn'd a Reverend Bishop-Man,
And what thou says with thy foul Mouth
Of *Paterson*, no Word is truth:
No Man on Earth was so prophane,
Except thy self whom all disdain.

  Thou monst'rous Map of all Transgression,
They're blind who blames a good Profession,
Tho' some who it profess be evil,
Thou art blind-folded by the Devil,
Who makes thee thus to vent thy self,
Since *Judas* he for love of Pelf,
Tho one of C. own Family,
He basely did his Lord betray:
Demas left the Faith of Christ,
(As thou *Dalryllian* Greedy beast)
For Greed of gain, yet none can blame,
For them the Christian Faith or Name.
But silly Dog thy Ignorance,
Makes thee to utter such Nonsense.
Yea Bishops were ordained to be,
By C. and his *Apostles* too.

  What though I find not *Dioikesis*
Nor Hierarchick *Kibernesis*
No more will thou find Sacrament
In the Old or New-Testament.
Yet we find what doth equalize them,
Which makes the Christian World to use them,
The twelve *Apostles* had more Power,
Than all the Christian World I'm sure;
They had both Power to bind and loose,
But blind Moles cannot judge of Hues:
To speak to thee of things Divine,
I cast but Pearls to the Swine.   Thou

Thou silly Ass no Man in Reason,
Can fix on me what's like to Treason,
If thou were not a senseless Sow,
Thou'd hang'd for Treason long ere now.
  Thou wretch of all Mankind most hateful,
Was thou not base and most ungrateful,
Unto *Dalrillian* who show'd thee Pity?
When thou was starveing at the City
Of *Edinburgh*, for lack of Bread,
When dighting Shoes was all thy Trade.
The Souter who at that time us'd thee,
Came seeking any Man to chuse thee,
He fied thee without thy consent,
And to *Dalrillian* North thee sent.
After thy starving in the South,
Dalrillians Praises fill'd thy Mouth,
As I have made thee to confess,
Thou monstrous Map of all Disgrace,
But beggars cannot bear of wealth,
Thou'll now disdain to drink his health,
But rails on him to thy disgrace,
Behind his back not to his face,
In's face thou dare not do the like,
Thou base unworthy Sutors Tyke.
  If I spell'd wrong why did thou not,
Reprove me first? Base blockish sot,
Which thou had done if thou had known,
An Error in mine, or thine own.
  Thou art a Monkey that doth strive,
To imitate what I contrive,
My way and Method; for the same,
I witness how thou writs thy Name;
Thy dull Brain knew no method how,
To write so neat more than a Sow;
The Lines which I made on *Glenshee*,
They were a Pattern unto thee,   Which

Which thou did borrow for that end,
Then *Judas* like thou did intend
Me to betray, thou hellish tyke,
No Heathen would have done the like
Thou'rt worse than *Judas* or the Devills,
Thou source of Sin and spring of Evils,
Go back unto the *Stygian* Coasts,
To thy Friends, the Infernal Ghosts,
And see if they will yet recruit thee,
Go tell them how I still confute thee.
Make haste again with limb and lith
And Sulphur spew at

Robert Smith.

Mr. *Craig* to Mr. *Smith.*

A N answer to that Damned Soul,
who in the mire of Sin doth roul,
and working still against the Light
Of Conscience Reason and of Right,
As he himself did testify,
before a Famous Company.
Into *Dalrillian*, for he said,
that he was very sore affraid,
that making Rhymes it was a Sin,
Yet he continues still therein,
And like his Master *Satan* roars,
Malicious words, which all abhores,
And still in shew of ugly Rhymes,
His Soul will perish for his Crimes.
　　The words bewray thine own Transgression,
As well as thou'd make clear Confession
If through the Mire thou did me lead,
I surely had a Drunken Guid,
For at that time the way was clean,
I there before had never been,　　　　else

else I would not have followed thee,
who was as full's the Ocean Sea.
　Thou says when I did Argument,
that meikle nonsense I did vent.
Thou lying dog I spoke good sense,
not as thou dost about *Nonens :*
Yea though I did Appologize,
I needed not to beg excuse.
The Reverence that I to him owe,
I by Submission ought to show.
　Though all thy Lies were real Truth,
thou'll quite thy challenge poor dull youth,
The Saints who lives upon the Earth,
are oftentimes so weak in Faith,
The real Truth for to attest,
Oaths are needful witless beast.
　Thou says that *Nonens* had a Being,
Which *Ens* alone is signifying,
Both *Ens* and *Nonens* are the same,
In thy account thou Map of shame,
thou contradicts the plainest Axioms
And do'st gainsay the chiefest Maxims,
The same to be and not to be,
Is an Impossibilitie.
　Yea in the Books which I did cite,
There are such words as I did write
Samuel Colvill mentions tricks,
Which are offensive to Mens P—ks,
he speaks of Ladys h—s of pleasure,
and of their circuit, and their measure,
Montgomery says he'll take the Taws,
And would therewith belt *Polwarts* B—s
Polwart in his reply again,
kiss the Cows C—t crys out right plain.
I on King *James* shall make no tarry,
but only shall propose a Querie　　　　　　Or

Or two ; to which make thou Reply,
And see if that prove Tyranny ?
What did he to his Royal Brother,
If that had been done by any other,
That's commonly alledg'd he did
He would have lost both Land and Head :
What way did he Lord *Essex* treat ?
How strove he for to Abrogat ?
The Penal Statutes, and erect,
his Chappels Papists to protect ?
How did he favour Church-mens Power,
When he inclos'd them in the Tower,
What kind of Method did he take,
When him his Forces did forsake ?
These Queries pray thee answer me,
and then from Tyranny him free.

 What tho' the *Apostles* had great Pow'r ?
(So hath the Church at this same hour)
None of them was above the rest,
Thou Ignorant and stupid beast :
the *Apostles* sure did Represent,
Christ's Church in the New-Testament,
Which consists in equality,
And not in Bishops Hierarchy.

 Thou ignorant and stupid Sow,
Though all that thou dost say were true,
No Man of common sense and Reason,
Can ever make thee free of Treason.
Since thou has such a great Relent,
At what's done by the Government :
If thou be wise than hold thy Peace,
Lest thou come off with great disgrace,
Thou begging came unto *Glenshee* ;
No Creature else would pity thee,
thou thankful was to them indeed,
for thee relieving in thy need :

         Thou

I

Thou wrote on them base Lies and tales,
What then ; thy tongue on some still rails.
   Go through *Braemare* descend to Hell,
And take the Devils word thy sell,
that thou needs more their help than ever,
the upper hand gain thou can never,
Begin anew strick with thy Pith,
And Blow thy Bellows silly *Smith*,
Thou'll do though thou rage like a Plague,
No injurie to
                                        Jasper Craig.

Smith to Craig.

A N answer to that silly brute,
    Who thinks in Rhyme for to dispute,
But when his Arguments him fails,
He falls in madness and he rails,
With hellish words which all abhores,
And terms obscene which he adores.
   And yet the Beast pretends to be ;
A great lover of Presbytrie,
Though each one knows they're not prophane ;
By what is seen by Mortal Men ;
That he from fools may get that name,
He strives the Bishops to defame ;
But silly Dog, if they had place ;
Thou would both call them Lord and Grace ;
Thou would both worship and adore them :
Though thou pretends now to abhore them :
But little worse are they or I,
Of all a stupid Brute can say,
Though thou rail till thy Lungs grow hoarse,
Our Fame is ne're a Pin the worse.
   Though thou ascribes to me Damnation,
Poor silly Dog thou wants Probation,   Was

Was it because I said that in,
Making of Lines, there wants not sin,
If thy best Works from sin be free,
There's none on Earth can equal thee;
Since Mens best Works are sinful; sure
Making of Lines cannot be pure,
Nor altogether free from sin,
Nor any Action Men Acts in.
My Verses whoso them compares,
To thy Devotion or Prayers;
They'll find they do them far exceed,
In every Point of what is good.
    Thou filthy beastly wretch all know,
Thou to all goodness art a foe,
Railing on Ladies, Bishops, Kings,
Such Songs to *Satan's* praise thou sings,
No marvel though thou rail at me;
Thou art a beast all persons see;
Thou knows thy Ears thou'rt like to lose,
Both for thy stinking Rhyme and prose;
Thou still reviles all sacred things,
And spits thy gall at Priests and Kings,
Whom all good Men will reverence,
But silly Dog thou'rt void of Sense,
Good *David* he did honour *Saul*,
And Bishops were ordain'd by *Paul*,
The holy Scripture doth advise,
Not to speak ill of Dignities.
    I bad thee show forth the Kings Crimes,
Thou said (into thy stinking Rhymes)
Were worse than *Saul's;* but silly fop,
Well doth thy Neck deserve the Rope:
Instead of showing, thou dost speer
His Crimes; thou base Son of a Whore;
For proof thou runs to common fame,
Which nothing's falser than the same;

I 2

A

A common Fame proves oft a Lye,
Thou sink of all iniquity;
What though he strove to abrogate;
The Penal Statutes what of that?
A Man to favour's own Profession,
Is sure in him no great transgression,
Thou Sink of Sin and all disgrace,
Thy Tongue can ne're his praise make less,
A Sow hates all sweet smelling things,
A websters brat here rails at Kings.
But let the Swine lick the Dung-hills,
And eat of Excrements their fills:
Base unclean Sow, grunt in the Mire,
Because it is thy sole desire;
It is for thee a fitter thing,
Than once to name a Queen or King.
  The Holy Bishops represent,
The Twelve *Apostles* Government:
The Stars which are in Heaven bright,
They are not all of equal Light;
Neither the Lights on Earth that be,
Are they of equal Dignitie.
The twelve *Apostles* had more pow'r
Than all the seventy had I'm sure,
Some were Prophets, some were Teachers,
Some Apostles, some were Preachers,
Paul caus'd the Churches make Collections,
For to supply the Poor's Defections,
He gave Commandments to the rest,
As his Epistles can attest.
This differs surely in degree,
And jumps not in Equalitie.
Base Dog thou can say now no more,
Though lately thou like Hell did roar
Against the Bishops and the King,
That thou might Satans praises sing.   Go

Go now keep silence hellish Swine,
Speak no more of these Men Divine,
I have them vindicated all,
From all that thou can write or rail.

Unworthy Beast all thou hast show'd,
Hath not thy ugly Dictions prov'd,
I'll scorn thy words here to rehearse,
To fyle my Pen, or stain my verse.

Yea even to be, and not to be,
Is no impossibilitie;
To be a blue and not be yellow,
May not this be thou brutish fellow?
Now where is all thy Logick now?
Thou Ignorant unlearned Sow.
Has thou of Logick any sense?
When I have beat thee with *Nonens.*

I came not begging to *Glenshee:*
The best of them they wrote for me,
To Mr. *Adam,* and *Dalmore,*
Into whose House I was before,
Because they heard my good repute;
I was not like to thee (a Brute)
That sent a Sutor seeking help,
To thee a stinking creashy Whelp,
Thou liv'd upon his Charity,
Till he was fain to shift for thee.

Now *Craig* thou'rt vanquish'd dead and gone,
Let this thy Tomb be write upon.

The Corps of *Craig* lies here in dust,
Stinking, Rotting in his Lust,
He was the Excrement of Evils,
And now he's gone to dwell with Devils:
Here lyes his Body as ye see,
The very dregs of Infamie,
Here let it ly; and stink in dust,
And's Name like *Judas* ay accurst.   But

But now behold how he goes to his post,
You'll see how he wins o're the *Stygian* Coast.

Craig *and* Charon, *When* Craig *comes to the River*
Styx.

Cr. O *Charon Charon.* hoy; come o're in haste,
That I may of the Pile of Brimston taste:
Ch. What are you? Or why do you so brag?
Cr. A hoy come o're 'tis poor *Jasper Craig ;*
Who lewdly liv'd while I liv'd Earth upon,
And now am come to possess my own.   (ploy?
Ch. What was your post? Or what was your Em-
Cr. I wallow'd in all sort of Earthly Joy. (King,
Ch. But you must tell what you've done for your
Then I in haste to him the word will bring.
Cr. I did concurr still to advance his Cause,
I oft broke G—s, but still I keept his Laws,
I Swore, I drank, I did carouse and lye ;
Yea I was guilty of Prophanity.
Ch. But did you nothing more at all but this?
Cr. I wallowed in all sort of Wickedness.
Who did me trust, I did them still betray ;
And *Judas* like I loved Money ay :
With *Cain* I strove my Brother for to kill,
I keep't my self from nothing that was ill.
And every one who to me good did shew,
I still to them more disaffected grew :
Go tell my Master I have acted more,
Than any that crost over here before.
       Charon goes to the Devil, and says.
   Ch. There is upon the Rivers other side,
One that's endu'd with horrid greed and Pride,
With Lust, Envy, and every other Crime,
That was commit since the first hour of time.
D. Go then, and see what post he will assume,
And I shall cause the great ones here make room.
                                      Ch.

Ch. Your Master speers what post you'll please to
Be ye be allow'd to cross the lake,   (take,
And you must also pay to me some hire,
Before I you admit to this Empire.
Cr. Go show my Master I'll content my sell,
With any post he'll give to me in Hell;
And when he's once acquainted well with me,
I hope by him I shall preferred be.
As for your hire I have a Crown which I
Ungrateful wone, my Charges to defray,
For which, I left him who did me most good,
Because I knew I was to cross this Flood.
Ch. Yone great advancer of your Kingdoms, he's
Content to take what ever post you please,
D. Go then in haste and bring him to this Region,
If he be fit, I'll set him over a Legion.
  Then *Charon* he sets on his flamming Oars, ⎫
Which in these Waters as the Thunder roars, ⎬
Until the Echo answers from the shores. ⎭
He first past *Lethe*, then throw *Styx* in flame,
And at the last to Drunken *Craig* he came.
In haste he in his vessel him receives, ⎫
And then unto the other side he drives; ⎬
And at the last in *Orcum* he arrives; ⎭
Where *Pluto* came, with him came *Proserpine*,
To welcome *Craig*, for him she'd never seen.
Which made his hair at first to stand upright
He was affrighted with this ghastly sight.
Then *Pluto* and *Proserpina* did make,
This sweet harangue, to this admitted snake.
  Infernal Powers who're all at our command,
Arise and take this fellow by the hand,
And let him have from every one his due,
And give him Bowls of Brimston till he spue:
And of my nectar; Tarr, with Rozen mixt;
And let him in the warmest room be fixt. This

This is the end poor *Craig* was treated with,
He'll spue no more his Gall at   *Robert Smith.*

Upon the Duke of Athols *Hunting,*
Where Men with Swords the Deer were dunting.

P*Arnassus* Mount and *Helicon* that fills
  Earth with your Fame, yield to *Atholian* Hills,
Your long retained praise, for surely they
Are worthy since they do you far outvy
For Mirth, for Game, Society and sport,
And pleasant Musick of the best Consort.
Mars and the Muses here at once they join,
The Muses only were but found in thine.
Our Hills *Parnassus* they do far outvy,
And strives t' exalt their tops above the Skye,
Here Noble Princes, and most Noble Lords,
As *Britain* can produce in her Records,
Are come to take their Recreation here,
And see the Sport, betwixt Men, Dogs, and Deer.
The Prince himself he is most meek and mild,
The Men are Martial, and the Deer most wild.
Which of the three, the other doth excell,
For Meekness, Manhood, Madness, who can tell?
The Prince in meekness, who can once compare ⎫
With him, or who can claim an equal share ? ⎬
None but these Nobles him associates here. ⎭
Noble *Douglass* of them leads the Ring,
With *Elcho, Gray,* and *Athol's* blest Off-spring,
Noble *Nairn,* and brave *Newton, Grahame,*
Meffon, Glenlyon, Ochtertyre by Name,
Yea many more whose Praises to rehearse,
Would fill whole Volumns & make endless verse
'Tis only great Games that great Souls can please,
'Tis below the lofty Eagle to catch flies,
They can endure Hardship, Fatigue and Toil,
And yet a Glory to the *British* Soil,   Like

Like *Athols* Souldiers, none in any Lands,
Quick, Swift, well hearted & most prompt in hands;
For surely if the Devil would appear,
They'd kill him in the likeness of a Deer, (them,
On Earth I'm sure there's none that can command
But their most Just, Illustrious Prince among them,
Long may their Glorious Prince live on their head,
And Heaven enjoy, when to this World has dead,
Atholian Hills, they'll Swear who have you crost,
You hold more Deer, than *Etna's* Flames could rost

POSTSCRIPT.

FRom Noble *Athol* I've received more,
    Than from all those e're got my Lines before:
For all the rest a Virtue has untold,
I Swear they are not Prodigal of Gold:
Let *Bacchus* Friends them Praise for sure *Apollo's*,
Can never call them Liberal or good Fellows.
For if my Pen shall turn as Sweir's their Purse,
I fear this is the last I'll write in Verse,
O *Athol* great! With Virtues all possest,
The Love of Gold is not in *Athol's* Breast.

F I N I S.

PART. II.

To the Memory of Mr. Alexander Campbell *sometime a Preacher,* Sed semper sine stipendio.

MIsfortunate in every thing,
    He hath been all his Life,
In Arms he rose against his King,
    For Stipend and a Wife;
But Gods just hand did him confound,
    And all Men did him hate,

K   But

For Providence hath cast him down
    Unto a low estate :
For he his own doth not possess,
    He Stipend never got,
He Preach't although he wanted Grace,
    Yet greed he wanted not.
He never car'd to feed the Flock,
    But he would fleece them fain,
Not Souls to Christ, but means a stock
    That he desir'd to gain.
Yet Providence him still keeps Poor,
    And under such disguise,
To every one he doth appear
    Madder far than wise.
He'll be no more a Puritan,
    They are not liberal ;
Nor will he be a Bishops man,
    Their Power is now so small.
But give him Gear and Worldly Pelf,
    His heart it is so evil,
He'd sell his Soul, Service and Self,
    With good will to the Devil.
Contentedly his hands would hold
    Poor Earth, for his abode ;
The Heavens, he would give for Gold ;
    For Worldly Pelf, his God.
But stay my Muse, go on no more ;
    It's but a silly jest :
Since thou of Subjects hast such store,
    Writ no more on a Beast.

A Reply to the same by Mr. Alexander Cambel *alias*
    Padaua, *Entituled thus,* To the Rifty Poet of
    Strahardle and *Glenshee.* Mr. *Robert Smith.*

H E whom thou rails at, begs thee still to write,
    Not out of friendship to be sure, but spite ;
                         For

For as a Piss-pot thrown with aukward force,
Against a Wall, returns upon its source;
Even so thy dull attempts missing their aim,
Brand with Disgrace, thy once bespotted Name:
For all that have thy nasty Verses seen,
Judge them the Product of a Beggers spleen.
So one wild Whore abandon'd to her shame,
And starv'd with hunger all Mankind doth blame,
Pinching in each dark corner of the streets,
Spits out her harmless gall on all she meets,
While mocking Crouds indifferently pass by,
And bids the useless wretch curse God and dye.

A Duply or another Satyr,
On Mr. Campbell *Mendicator.*

IS *Balaams* Ass again become alive?
That did this nonsense (verse) contrive?
But she did speak with much more witt,
A larger share she had of it,
Than *Padaua* that wrote this Verse,
And sent them me to wipe my A—s
  Thou begs of me that I may write,
I think a Beast deserves not spite;
And if I to thee favour show,
I cast but Pearls to a Sow.
  Thou bears the name of a Divine,
But lives a life like Dogs or Swine;
Of Wonders it was not the least,
That they should graduat a Beast.
  Thou calls my Verses, Beggers Spleen,
Which I am not as may be seen,
I have an honest occupation,
Becoming both my Name and Station;
But thou still begs, as all Men knows,
Thy stock would scarce maintain thee brose,

K 2

And

And pinching hunger doth thee press,
Because thou eats to such excess,
As would ashame Mankind to see,
Or sit with thee for gluttonie.
　Thou says I Rail (behind my back)
Because of thee the Truth I spake,
Thou with thy own Tongue did confess,
That all Men said thou wanted Grace.
Thou said thou was a Puritan,
Only for greed of worldly gain;
So these Premisses do make good,
The Lines wherewith I did conclude.
　When we were face to face, thou knows,
Thou durst not speak in verse or prose,
Thou Sot, thou's tane these three Months time
To set thy base nonsense in Rhyme,
And yet expressions thou dost use,
Which would affront a Poets Muse.
　No marvel at the Preaching Trade,
Though thou could never gain thy Bread,
Thou Whorish, Drunken, Godless Glutton,
For Beer and Wine, for Beef and Mutton,
For Aquavity, Ale and Brandy,
Thou'd call thy self the Devils *Sandy*,
And would for ever with him dwell,
Into the lowest Pit of Hell;
But Drink and Eat while thou art here.
For there thou wilt get harsher cheer,
Even bowls of Brimston from the Lake,
Whereof all Drunkards do partake,
But hold Pen: As I said before,
Upon a Beast writ thou no more.

　　To Mr. Campbel *and his Associats.*
Ｂ Ut if some other drunken Ass,
　Has tane thy part, me to minace,　　　　I

I value not your Brain-sick heads ;
I scorn your favours, begs your feads
Though both your Bullets fly like showers,
I'll make my Pen raise up new Towers,
Me to defend from all your shots,
You Idle, Drunken, Brain-sick sots,
Ye make my Pen gust in my Nose,
That I'm necessitat to close.

In Imitation to Montrose *Lines on K.* Ch. *the* 2d. [1st]

IF I had Pens in number as the sand,
If Seas were Ink, and every herb a hand,
Though years I liv'd million of millions told,
And had the Genius of an Angel bold :
Pens, Ink and Hands, yea, time, and all would
Before I could thy worthy Merites tell.   (fail,

An Acrostick upon a young Man who desired to be
made Famous by Verse any way.

CHurlish, Greedy, Ignorant and Vain :
Hugging Earth, despising Heavenly Gain ;
An Excrement of Earth, to Heaven hateful,
Regards not Man, to God ungrateful ;
Loving to be for folly Cannoniz'd,
Endangering his soul, with Whores abus'd,   }
So he may wish he had not been Baptiz'd.   }
   Small in Vertue, great in every Vice,
Much given to Lying, Cursing, Cards and Dice,
A Man that loves to be cry'd up for Evils,
Longing to be a Fiend among the Devils.

To the Tune of the Earl of Aboyne.

WHat is it that can move the Hearts of Men to
These things which are transitory,   (Love
                                                     For

For those that highest be, them presently we see,
    Divested of all their Glory.
This World that I see now present to mine eye,
    It is all turn'd round in a motion,   (to rave,
Even as the wind doth blow, and makes the Seas
    Raising storms in the Ocean.   (Debts,
For those that have Estates, are most enthral'd in
    What Pleasur's in all their glory,
The fool oftimes enjoys the labour of the wise,
    This World is so transitory.
Do we not see the great to covet the Estate,
    Of the Poor that's far below them,
And them they do envy, because at home they stay
    Though they be providing to them. .
The poorer sort they say how happy are they,
    That lives in Pomp and in Honour,
And every one envys, what Providence denies,
    And grudges at his Donor.   (the field,
The great ones will not yield their hands to plow
    But for Honour still they're aspiring,   (Gold
The Lawyers Tongues are sold, for Money and for
    Still getting, and still desiring.
O happy thrice is he, if any such there be,
    Whose Contentment exceeds his treasure,
And whose lot is such, as not to covet much,
    But in what he hath, takes Pleasure.
Diogenes he had more pleasure in his shade,
    Than he that all the World enjoyed.
In peace he laid him down, and quiet sleep he found
    And of no Man he was envyed.   (sires;
Alexander's vast Empires they breed him vast de-
    He had all things, yet not contented, (Lord,
Which the Earth could afford to him that was her
    And for lack of more Worlds he lamented.
I'd rather join with *Pan* for to be a rustick Swain,
    Than to be a Peer of the Nation,

                              For

For to feed my Flocks, on the Mountains & Rocks,
   And be freed from all vexation :
With *Diana* I will sing, and sport me in the spring
   And will go with the Nymphs a huntings
And there we will behold our pleasures manifold
. In the Valleys, as in the Mountains. (appears,
In the spring of the year when the tender grass
   And all the Herbs are a springing, (Flowers,
Then we will strew our Bowers about with pleasant
   And recreat our selves with singing. (do abound
We'll hear the Rocks resound, with the Birds that
   Whose voices are as pleasant Musick ;
And round about our Bowers ther'll spring the plea-
   Which are all most fit for Physick. (sant flowers
Ambition, wrath nor hate, shall not trouble my Estat
   Though I be of the meanest station, (Wives,
Then I'll laugh at the lives of those opprest with
   Though they were the Peers of the Nation.

To the Tune of Katharin Oggie.
YOu Muses all both great and small
    Assist my Pen, the matter,
It is so bright, makes me delight
To praise this comely Creature.
Into whose face is such a grace,
I cannot but admire her,
Her other Parts with Wits and Arts
Make me so much desire her,

         2.
There is no Muse that would refuse
To yield unto this Creature.
No man on Earth that draweth breath,
Is able to draw her stature
The Goddesses in their finest dress,
Must all bow down before thee
Apollo sings thy praise on strings,
And all the Gods adore thee.   *Ve-*

3.

Venus fair makes no compare
With thee, for all her beauty,
Rich *Juno* she must yield to thee,
Although both Proud and haughty,
Mercurius would surely blush,
For to speak out before thee,
Minerva sayes thou's win the Prize,
Says *Orpheus* I'll adore thee.

4.

Yea all the gods and goddesses
They do most highly prize thee,
The Raggs of meanness though on thee,
They cannot all disguise thee,
Yea, *Crœsus* Pelf with thy sweet self,
Comes not in competition ;
More than the Reigns and Crowns of Kings,
I covet thy fruition.

5.

Her Eyes are as the brightest Skys,
Or Stars into *December*,
They ravish me when I them see,
The goddesses attend her.
The sweetest Flowers in *Ceres* Bowers,
Her breath doth far surpass them.
Her Properties and Elogies
There's none that can express them.

6.

If't were my fall or fortunes call,
To pass through *Ætnas* burnings,
I could make chuse without refuse,
Thy thoughts could repel Mournings,
The roaring Seas I'd not refuse
To cross or venture for thee,
The proudest waves or *Neptuns* jaws,
Should not my heart make sorry.

If

7.

If as much Land I could command,
Or Men as *Alexander*,
When I thee see, I could make thee
More than the half Commander ;
Renouned she of all may bee,
She's the Diadem of Beauty,
And to set forth her matchless worth,
She's neither Proud nor haughty.

8.

No created brain, nor *Cherubs* Pen,
Can praise thee Right nor fitly,
Nor any Muse that Man can chuse
Can thee describe compleatly,
Whom all admires and much desires,
Can I but truly love thee ?
And wish to thee Prosperity,
That Fate may never move thee.

Upon the viewing of the stately Palace of Glams,
Extempore.

ILlustrious *Lyon* in *Angus-shire* doth dwell,
  Into a Palace which others all excell,
It's Buildings sure none can on Earth define ;
Mimus no more, nor *Momus* can Repine ;
If they it saw, they surely would desire,
To see it more, for all do it admire.
Into the midest of that Shire it lys :
And far excels them all for Rarities,
It Curious Works on every side doth grace,
Such as are seen into no other place,
'Twixt it and others, there is as great odds,
As is betwixt frail Mortal Men and Gods.
Too vast a Subject its for *Ovids* Pen,
Or *Virgils* Stile : or the most Learned Brain :

L   To

To write, to paint, or set it rightly forth,
According to it's beauty and it's worth.
I do believe, the Gods have built the same,
For none on Earth is able once to Name,
Far less descrive it's matchless worth aright,
Which is so glorious, splendid, shining, bright:
There, all may see the great wonders of Arts,
Without, within, and round on all its parts.
Particulars, I do not here descrive,
But them I will to the Beholders leave,
Who may behold, what would great Volumns fill
But are too high a Subject for my quill.
It is too great for any Subject, save
For him and his, who builded it so brave,
It's Loyal Lord is sprung of Ancient Kings,
Whose Royal Off-spring over our Lands yet Reigns
I wish his House and Off-spring ever be
On Earth Renoun'd, unto Eternitie:
And when the course of this frail Life doth end,
His Name and Glory, farer may extend;
Even far above the Lucid Stars and Sky,
And live in Heaven throughout Eternity.

Upon Writing with the Left hand, Extempore.
I Wish the Left-hand try'd to write,
  As with that Brain I alwise dite,
I've quot the Left, and tane the Right,
I'd change my Brain so, if I might.

Upon the Consideration of the Stars.
W Hen I behold the Lucid Stars of Light,
  With sparkling Rays, bright shining in the
My Soul is ravish'd when I meditate,   (Night,
On his great Power who did those Bodys creat;
 .Those glorious Creatures Dance, Run & Rejoice,
To serve their Master in the Ætherial Skyes.   No

No Rest, no sloth, no slow delay possess
Those Lucid Vessels, in their foreward race ;
Each one his rank in perfect order keep,
And some doth watch, when others seem to sleep.
No Emulation nor Envy they know,
Unlike to us, vile Miscreants below,
The mean envys the Grandour of the High,
Yea few's content with what they do enjoy,
Not so above, for there they all accord,
In perfect peace to serve their Holy Lord :
Each one's content with what he doth possess,
A Joy is seen to sparkle in each ones Face,
They serve their God, they grudge not nor demur
No hate from Heaven nor Earth do they incur,
They through thick darkness do their light display
Till fair *Aurora* Ushers in the day,
And *Sol* their Prince begins for to appear,
And bids those watchful Sentinels retire
He then his light throughout the Earth doth spread
With blushing face to have lyn so long a Bed.

Upon the Honourable David Spalding *of* Ashentully.

D*Avid* he was for Meekness Grace and Worth,
Above the Learn'dest Pen to set him forth.
Valiantly he *Israel* did Govern,
In things both good and bad he did discern,
Doubtless thou didest from this *David* Learn.
Sweet, Loving, Meek, may sure thy Motto be
Put out thy Arms in Books of *Heraldrie*,
A generous sp'rit thou hast, a pleasant grace,
Loving to help all who are in Distress,
Delighting still in Mercy, Peace and Love
In all thy Deeds all base things thou'rt above,
Nothing that's vile can harbour in thy breast,
Guile, Fraud, Deceit, to thee's no welcome guest

Love, Honesty, Peace and Truth is the aim,
At which thou levels still with might and main
In every thing thou shows thy self to be,
Righteous, and from all Malice free,
Delightful *David* sure belongs to thee,
On Vice the gates of thy pure heart are shut
For evermore, and they away are put.
A generous Soul to all what's good inclin'd,
Shows forth thy worth as doth thy loving mind,
Honour attend thee, Piety support thee,
Eternal Mercy let it alwise fort thee.
No Hate, Envy, does thou to any bear,
Thou loves all Mankind, and thy God dost fear:
Unmov'd for ever let thy Familie
Live and abound, in Peace and Sanctitie.
Long may it stand, and greater may it grow 〉
In Vertue, and with all goodness flow, (Dew. 〉
Even as the Plants that're blest with Heav'ns 〉

S Ince fickle fortune she,
     Upon me frowns,
And I'm in miserie,
Thou me disowns.
          Yet still I wish to thee
          All Health, Prosperitie,
          And will for ever be
                    Thy slave in Bonds.
     For me I must confess,
I am too vile
In thy Heart to find place,
Or have a smile,
          From that sweet Lips of thine,
          Where Rose like Colours shine,
          Thy Breath excells the Wine
                    O sweetest soil.
Into thy comely Face,   All

All Beauty shine,
Decked with such a grace,
Sure it's Divine :
    Where *Venus* doth display,
    Her Features only gay,
    Which makes my sp'rits to say,
          O if't were mine.
  But I cannot show forth,
Nor can I praise
Thy surly matchless worth,
My Senses maze,
    Although thou me abhore,
    I'll love thee more and more,
    And alwise thee adore
          And glory raise.
  Yea though I pine away
For love of thee,
My Tongue shall ever say,
My Dear is shee,
    And shall be Day and Night
    Her I'll love with my might,
    And therein will delight
          Until I die.
  I ever shall Rejoice,
When I shall hear
That thou makes happy choise,
My dearest dear,
    Although thy love me kill,
    And thou should hate me still
    I'll never wish thee ill
          O matchless Peer,
  When I hear of thy grief,
I'll bear a part
Though that be small relief
To thy sweet heart,
    Yet while thy Heart is sad

Then

Then mine shall not be glad,
It's be in sorrows clad
   And feel Griefs smart
 Thy slave with weeping Eyes
Bids thee farewell,
In bitter grief he crys,
And pains doth feel :
  Therefore I bid adue
  My dearest dear to you,
  My love shall ay be true
   And firm as steel.

A Satyr on [a] *Presbyterian Supplicant, for Swear-*
ing contrar Oaths.

ALL you that Lovers are of Sport,
 Come all and unto me resort ;
And I unto you all shall tell,
Of one that's riding post to Hell,
And's making haste with might and speed
For to pass over the *Stygian* Flood,
To *Charon* he will be a cross ;
If he bring over *John Burnets* Horse,
The Cause why this I let you see,
Is for his Oaths of Perjury,
It is well known unto you all,
Although to you I should not tell,
That he did swear in *Banchory's* School,
That *Brown* pusht not with Durk nor Tool,
But soon he goes to *Edinburgh*,
And there did Swear another Oath.
When he came there he gott a Wigg,
And then he ceas'd to be a Whigg,
And with the Wigg he got a Hat,
Which made him swear he knew not what :
He pretends to drink no Wine or Ale,
But for eight pounds *Scots* his Soul did sell.
     Which

Which *Inchmairly* gave *John Hunter* less,
Because his Soul he could not stress.
Good Sir, if ye'd kept up your purse,
This Man had been fred from the Curse,
O Man ! Thy Conscience has been wide
The fear of God thou's laid aside,
Which thou and every one may see,
To Swear Oaths of Contraritie,
All you that Lovers are of Christ,
I pray with him keep no more tryst,
Except it be to bring him in,
To see a sight of his great sin ;
For Christ himself bids us beware
Of Wolfs that Wedder Skins do wear.
Which ye may see they're of that stock,
That's forsaken Christ and's little flock ;
With *Demas* he's forsaken *Paul*,
Though to the ruin of his Saul ;
But Prayers long he will not want,
Though he of Charity be scant.
He thinks not meikle of this grace,
In his Opinion it wants place.
With *Jehu* he'll show his great zeal,
That all his faults he may conceal,
He'll go from this to *Aberdeen*,
At Sacraments for to be seen ;
And as though there he got it nought,
Straight on he marches unto *Eight*,
Ere it be done he'll have't at *Skeen*,
As it before he'd never seen ;
At *Clunie* he right soon will be,
And at *Kincragielesly* too ;
And from this, he'll have't at *Birss*,
And sure he will not miss't at this ;
If one *Strahan* once a Pastor had,
Of that this Man would be right glade ;   That

That he might get some Bread and Wine,
And after that a little Coin.
Yea at *Midmar* he will not scar,
The Sacrament he will have there,
By this he'll view the Presbytrie,
Except four, up the Water of *Dee.*
Good Ministers if ye keep back
Your Silver, this Mans Heart will break,
And happ'ly run to dispair,
And cease a Whigg to be Mair.
Good Minister I pray you now,
To take good heed what ye do,
If Ignorants ye do debar,
I pray you of this Man bewar.
Therefore let him be set apart,
Till God break in upon his Heart,
Hypocrite's of so small a threed,
That few can know if it be good,
Therefore take ye the better tent,
See if in heart he do relent,
Let not Religion more be stain'd,
Nor yet God's holy Name prophan'd,
Many Religion makes the Cloak,
The sacred Name of God to mock,
But if this he intends to do,
He'll perish sure eternallie ;
And with *Judas* he'll keep tryst,
Who for Money sold's Master Christ,
And now in Prison he is fast,
Though back the Money he did cast ;
And so will he ere long be there,
If he go on false Oaths to Swear.
No more I'll add no more I'll say,
But leave him till the Latter Day,
When he must give account for all,
And so to you I bid farewell.   An

An Answer to a Letter in mock to the People of Brae-
marr, *giving an account of the Country and Gentlemen thereof.*

THE last from *Birss* I did receive,
  Makes me believe they're turn'd to rave,
Because they spoke of Monsters here ;
With us no such thing do appear.
And did nor *Cato* me advise,
I could you argue otherwise :
Therefore such things I will not use,
Nor yet my Country scandalize,
But of this place I shall you tell,
It is right pleasant where I dwell.

Here in the place of my Repose,
  I want not Friends I fear not Foes :
Much I delight here to abide ;
By us the Rivers swiftly glyde.
In motion swift they will not stay,
Untill your Country they pass by,
And still they're restless in their motion,
Till they're disbog'd into the Ocean.
Every well spring in motion goes,
Till it in *Thetis* lap repose.
Also the Hills here us they hedge,
With mighty Rocks and stony *Craigs,*
Where Connies sleep and make their Beds,
With *Birsy* Goats, and wanton Kids.
Also the Woods they us surround ;
Where Birds do make a pleasant sound,
And with their Voices sweetly sing,
And doth extoll their God and King,
Who did them create ; they with their Tongues,
Sweet praises to him give in Songs :
  M   They

They in the Branches sing most sweet,
When sinful Man is fast asleep:
Although they have no count to give,
They praise their maker while they live.
Here likewise spacious Forrests are,
To feed Roe-Bucks and fellow Deer;
The Meads are plenteous of sweet grass,
To feed both Heifers, Stags, and Horse.
We've Gardens here with Flowers full bright,
Which to the smell is great delight;
Here grows tall Firrs where builds the Storks,
(With limber Twiggs and slender Birks)
Whose lofty tops to Heaven they raise,
With mighty Winds makes dreadful noise.
As brick was thick into *Jerus'lm*,
When overthrown by *Vespasians* Son:
So in this place here lies tall Trees,
When once *Æolus* angry flees;
When in his rage he wanders Woods,
And throws tall Trees in running Floods,
He makes them here in heaps to ly,
When he rides angry through the Sky:
But for his feed we care not much,
The station of our dwellings such,
That he can do us little harm,
Though he his Captains four should arm,
For *Notus* he cannot us heat,
For Hills which are before our gate;
And though *Aquilo* rise in rage;
He must go back by force of Craigs.
Favonius with his thundering Voice,
Cannot approach us with his force,
Nor *Subsolanus* us affright;
Mountains surround us of such hight.
Though each of those his Brother implore,
Yet for their feeds we care no more,   Than

Than Wolfs for Number of the Flocks ;
Or sharpest Ax for hardest Oaks.
Vulturnus we can laugh and scorn,
For *Boreas* we shall not mourn,
Nor can *Caurus* make us affraid,
Though he in rage were never so mad ;
Though *Africus* comes in great storms,
He knows not where to set his arms,
Therefore he's forced back to turn,
Because he meets but with a scorn.
As for the People here that dwell,
Their Praises I can scarcely tell,
For they in virtue are so rare,
I none with them can well compare.
Our Gentlemen are all well bred,
Endued with Grace, emptied of Pride,
Hates nastiness in every thing,
And still they're Loyal to their King.
Here are fair Ladys in this place,
Of Virtue full, endued with Grace,
Whom *Solomon* doth better praise,
Than what my Thoughts can here devise.
The vulgar sort I leave to fame,
I no more here shall speak of them,
Which if I did, I could not miss,
This Country for to scandalize.

Upon a Whore Extempore.

THis wanton Whore this many a year,
  Hath play'd the Loun about her,
And now at last, all shame she's past,
And tane on *Robie Cowper*.

A Letter written from Braemar, to his dear Come-rade in Birss, Alexander Ross.

THis Country now wherein I live,
  I cannot well express,

Nor

Nor can I to you rightly give,
An account of their address,
It's not of Gentlemen I mean,
Nor of them do I write,
For they are right in fashion seen,
In Country, Land and street.
   But for to see our vulgar sort,
In all their rich array,
It would afford you jest and sport
Till you were like to dy.
To you I'll give a view of them,
Even such as I did take,
To every one it is great shame,
That wants a Highland Feake;
Behold and see their prettie Feet,
Adorn'd with upland shoes,
Yet he is never a Man compleat,
Till he get Tartan Trews:
With a Bullet bag upon his belt,
To hing upon his Thigh,
With a rusty Durk and Iron Hilt,
To come beneath his Knee.
O happy's he who can command,
A Horn for his Powder,
With a sooty Gun into his hand,
Or else upon his Shoulder,
Then on the Kirk he's fit to go,
For to hear a Preachment;
But he must have a Sword also,
For its a great Impeachment
Upon his Honour, who hath not
A measure for his Powder,
That he aright may measure his shot,
And it hings over his Shoulder,
Than their Teeth, somes Hair is much more short,
Their Luggs a large span lang,   Whom

Whom to behold it is good sport,
When they make a harangue ;
Each of them some Ribbons hath,
Red mixt with black or blue,
He thinks he's in his Highland Graith,
When it hings over his Brow.
They care not for the Summer heat,
Nor for the Winter cold,
If that they can get Cheese to eat
With Butter and good Phoal,
On Sabbath some to Church goes,
And others to the Glen,
For to see their Cows and Ews,
And feed on Curds and Cream,
Others some doth back Jucks take,
For to hear their Priests,
Then to the Virgin down they beck,
With Crosses on their Breasts ;
With Holy Water they begin,
I wish ye had a part,
To purify your Soul from Sin,
And sanctify your Heart
Beads they adore with Images ;
And then makes their Confession,
Unto the Priest that says the Mass,
Then they get a Remission,
All of them doth Robbery know,
Since *James* the Seventh's Reign,
But they have suffered meikle woe,
Since *ANN* became their Queen.
Here Honesty was much cry'd down,
Even in the Days of old ;
But Law hath now forc'd every Clown,
To take him to some hold.
Sore is their Hearts that they must gain
Their Bread by sweat of Brows,

If't

If't had remain'd as it began,
They'd liv'd on stoll'n Cows.

POSTSCRIPT.

With slushing and souching,
Each one his Cutty reeks,
They care not, nor spare not,
The Cold for want of Breeks.

*Upon two young Gentlemen, supposing them both to
be in Love with a young Lady: Written Extempore.*

TWo Gentlemen this day,
  They went to *Invercal,*
And there they did espy,
A Beauty, though not tall.
  Each one his eyes he fixt,
Into this Beauties Face,
Yet sure no Love betwixt,
The Rivals in this case,
Says *Garthanmoir,* I'll dy
Sure, if she me refuse,
Quoth *Tulloch* so will I ;
If me she do not chuse.
And then like Tods on Cleiks,
They star'd each others face,
Each one her Love he seeks
Into this woful case.
Each thought within himself,
How shall I gain her Love ?
I'd disdain worldly Pelf,
That she would loving prove.
But for Love, *Garthanmoir*
He yielded up his Breath,
His Rivals heart was sore,
And like to die that Death :
No Beer nor Ale he could,
No not so much as Taste,

For

For her in Beauties mould,
That was so neatly cast.
Quoth he, when I reflect
Upon *Anne Barclays* face !
And her cheerful aspect,
O ! for her sweet solace !
I could most willing be,
Though I had all the Earth,
To give it all to thee,
When I but smell thy breath ;
But if thou me refuse,
Then presently I'm gone,
Therefore I pray make chuse
Of him, whose heart's thine own,
But's Passion being strong,
No longer could endure,
What ever was his wrong,
No Doctor could him cure.
Therefore let both be laid
Into one Tomb inclos'd
Of them it shall be said,
Here's two, that one but chos'd,
And so they do deserve
To have an Epitaph
Wrot in a stone to serve,
Which age may not wear off,
   Here into this House of Clay,
Two great Lovers, (Grants) *do ly,*
Who for one Lass their Bloods could spend,
And she of both hath made an end.

Upon their Comerads who mocked them, Because
they fell in Love.

FOur Gentlemen, (two had brown Horse)
   Went to convoy the Laird of *Luss,*

I spoke to two of them before ;
Robert remains yet, and *Remoir;*
(All the four are called *Grants,*
Yet two of them are scarcely Saints,)
Of this two I think indeed,
They'll do no ill, as little good :
Yea take them both in the complex,
I can them reckon of no Sex :
That they're not Men, they plainly prove,
Because uncapable of Love ;
That they're mad fools who Loves none,
I witness sapient *Solomon,*
Who had more Wisdom than all Kings,
Yet Women lov'd above all things.
They are not of the other sort,
Their Beards are long, which should be short.
But what they are, Ill tell you plain,
They're Animals in shapes of Men,
But if they would the finest prove,
They must implore the gods of Love,
And see, if they can by their fires
Or Charmes enflame their dull desires.
But if they will not then they must,
Just as they are go to the Dust :
Their Epitaphs must neither be,
A Satyr, nor an Elegie.
　Here lies two, they're both now Dead,
Of none had neither Love nor Feed,
Because they were worth no Mans pains,
Having neither Hearts nor Brains.
How both are now, and how both fares,
There's none that knows and as few cares.

　Upon an Old Horse of Dalmoirs Extempore.
*D*Almoir surely ye may rejoice,
　Because your Men they made good choise

In buying such a Horse :
His Maik is not in all *Braemar*,
He's neither gaady, wood nor scar ;
   Yet like *Bucephalus.*
And now your Men have brought him home,
For to trail in some Stones,
He is a Nagg both wise and tame,
As good as goes on bones.
With groaning and moaning,
He's brought stones from the Hill ;
With Rugging and drouging,
Your Yard-Dyke up to fill.
Ye've sent him now to *Alloway*,
With a burden neither light nor sma,
   Unto the Earl of *Marr ;*
If ye go on to treat him so,
To him ye will breed meike woe,
   Therefore I pray beware,
To use ay and abuse ay
Your Horse at such a rate,
For Danceing and prancing,
He is a Nagg most neat.
Duke *Hamilton* had been right glade.
This Horse for to command,
The Parliament, with him, to ride,
Among the Noble Band.
   His Lot I fear was never such,
To have his Maik into his Coach,
   So slender and so lean,
He's lived so long, I think indeed,
His Days have been before the flood,
   And in the Ark's been tane.
For Riding he doth far excell,
All that are in this place,
Although he want both Mane and Tail,
He's fit to run a Race,
      N   His

His teeth then, forsooth then,
They sit out through his Lips,
His Eyen Sir, they seem Sir,
To go back to his Hips.
I fear his Bons will cut the skin,
And look out to the Air,
This many years, his Teeth doth grin,
On him I'll not write mair.

*The following Lines were given to me by way of
  a Letter,* (at the Colledge of Aberdeen) *but no
  person would own to be their Author; But the
  Bearer told me, that the Author was content to
  enter into a Carminal fight, though it should last
  seven years.*   He thus begins.

Sir, when your Fame at first did reach mine Ears,
  I was surpriz'd with fool Phantastick Fears,
I did believe, and partly yet believes,
You are the foremost Poet now that lives.
While it was said, that ye could still off hand,
On any Subject make verse at command,
At all times, and good verse too :
I do believe none can do't, save't be you.
For as a Man endu'd with noble Parts,
Perhaps is Master of some Trades and Arts,
Yet sure he cannot use them all at once,
More than a teethless Wife can gnaw hard bones:
For in a River as we plainly see,
How soon and oft the waters changed be,
Yet still goes on like *Phœbus* Beams,
By the Succession of new fruitful streams ;
I think Mans Brain was ne'er ordain'd,
That only one thing there should be contain'd.
But all your verses that e're I saw,
Doth not deserve so meikle dread or aw,   As

As I at first did give unto your name,
So highly blowen by the trump of fame ;
I offer this to let you see
There's one beside your self, that will you dare
To open face, and will not at you scare,
To try and see your so much praised strain,
And what's the product of your stinking Brain ;
And since I've made the first assault let you,
Choose a fit Subject which we may pursue
So I give over your answer till I see,
Take this in haste from honest *Tam* go free.

The Answer, but not of my composing at first.

SIr shiteing I receiv'd your Letter,
   The more I read, I shite the better.
The ground was clean and void of grass,
Your Letter serv'd to wipe my A—se.

The Unknown Authors Answer.

THou ugly filthy senseless sot,
   How durst thou ever Paper blot ?
With such a foul beshitten Letter,
I had it seen if thou'd had better,
How well guest I thy nasty brain
To be but stinking ; while its strain
Delights in no Poetick Art,
But making two'r three Lines on Dirt.
Thy verse well shows what kind thou art,
A Poet sure not worth a fart :
And scarcely can thou spell one word ;
Thy Scholarship's not worth a Turd :
I'll never sure more to thee write,
For making of thy self beshite,
I fear the Maid that dights thy Breeks,
Will curse me with Tears on her Cheeks,

N 2   So

So fare thou well thou silly beast,
I wish thou be not at a Feast,
When thou my Letter doth receive.
In case thy Back-side misbehave.

To the Unknown Authors or Author.

UNworthy Knaves, base silly Sots ;
   I have perus'd your Rhymes ;
Which brings upon you stains and blots,
That ye've deny'd your Names :
Ye Paper-blotters with nonsense,
Without all ground or Reason,
Among us ye your Lines disperse ;
Yet's feared for them as Treason.
Ye boast, and brag most furiously,
Yet fears your Names to show ;
The same to me it doth imply,
Your Face is like a Sow ;
And it show great shame ye think,
Your Snowts with dirt are fyl'd,
No Marvel though your Brains did stink,
When ye your Lines compyl'd.
Ye are more fit dry-stools to toom,
Than to write Elegies :
Let never more your verse be seen,
All Poets you refuse.
At first when I thy Letter got,
Had it been worth my pains,
I had it answer'd to a mot,
And never vext my brains :
Its neither in thy Brain nor Power,
To make Elegie or Satyr,
And like a Fox thou love's to lower,
Because thou has no matter.
O fy ! Think shame, and turn thy back ;
Thy face cannot be seen :

I say, go back with shame and lack,
Thou Sow of *Aberdeen.*
No Man on Earth hath ever hear'd
Of such a silly slave,
Who thinks to make himself admir'd,
And yet a new Name crave.
Thou Son of Hell that's angry at
The Gifts given to another :
Of thy Father *Satan* thou takes that,
Or *Erynnis* that's thy Mother.
There's none that hears thy verse or words,
Can thee a Poet Name,
To beat thy Brain with stink and Turds,
O fy ! Look black for shame !
The Muses they would surely blush,
To hear thy stinking strain,
Beware *Apollo* do thee crush.
For th' Product of the Brain.
For such a Rascal to Revile
All others with stout words ;
At him all Men may laugh and smile,
Whose Subjects is but T—ds :
If any think to turn the chase,
And say that I began,
I'll prove they lie into their face,
Where's their Honour then ?
Thou silly Dog at the first time,
(I tell't to thy Disgrace)
When I receiv'd thy senseless Rhyme
To dare me to my face,
Thou was so fear'd, thou turn'd a Liar,
And then deny'd thy name,
Though thou got neither gain nor hire,
O such a horrid stain !
That ever one who was Baptiz'd
Should turn a Mahomite,   (And

(And have his Senses so abus'd)
For senseless Rhyms to write.
Thou silly sot, what was thy drift?
At first when thou began?
Thy Fame and Honour to uplift,
Yet rose not half a span.
As thou at first deny'd thy Name,
Thou likewise did thy verse,
And for them both thou's got a stain,
Unto thy sad Disgrace.
Thou makes my Pen gust in my Nose,
Therefore I must leave off:
But yet I think before I close,
I'll write thy Epitaph.

How soon thy Breath is from thee gone,
And Death hath clos'd thine Eyes;
Let this be written on thy Tomb,
Here Dirts descriver lyes:
Who so delighted while he liv'd
Of Dirt to write and tell,
And with all goodness he was griev'd
Therefore he went to Hell.

Upon a Snuff-Mill.

TO all whose presents these perchance may come
    But most to *Balfour, Ogilvy, and Tomb,*
I by these presents show my Crime and Theft,
To gain my Point it was my nearest shift.
    Not long ago at *Spittel* of *Glenshee,*
It happen'd that Old *Tomb* did me,
As sundries do, we chanc'd to take a glass,
And in 'tis rear a snichen soon took place:
With *Tomb* I did a curious Mill espy,
On which my heart almost fell with my eye;
To have her I would truly be content,
Though I at large another groat had spent:

All

All would not do, no Money nor reward,
Tomb did the Gift and Giver so regard :
He still deny'd, made nice and looked sower,
Because he had her from the Laird *Balfour*,
He still made this his sole denying clause,
I'll ever keep her for the givers cause.
In the next place he did her much regard,
Her maker being Mr. *John Balvard;*
For both their sakes I still desir'd her more,
Than ever I had a Snichen-mill before.
Th' more he deny'd her, still the more I sought,
But all the while I spent my Breath for nought.
Then, her at last I did resolve to steal
But Honesty could not my Crime conceal,
Therefore I here to all Men it reveal,
My Prize obtain'd I took a sudden flight,
Since, of the Mill *Tomb* never got a sight.

   Sir, to you and all I've made Confession,
Next of her Maker I will seek Remission,
I'll Pennance dree in something less or more,
If he keep in that galling word, *Restore;*
Which if he bid, I'll hold me as before.

   Sir, if ye but confer on me this alms,
(Her Maker being Minister at *Glams*)
At greater length perhaps another time,
I may come for to give you thanks in Rhyme,
Which I have larger far than Coin or Gold,
The woeful Proverb this makes true to hold,
That Poets still are poor and needy,
As likewise this, that Kirk-men ay are greedy ;
And yet good Sir, if time and place permit,
A Snichen good ye may have out of it.

   Sir, if on *Tomb* ye look with but a frown,
And me reveal 'l may yet loose my own,

                    There-

Therefore ye'll let him from Rebuke pass free,
Thereafter he I hope will pardon me.

Sir,
I remain with all my Pith,
Your humble Servant Robert Smith.

Balfours *Answer to Mr.* Robert Smith.

SIr, I have yours, in which you beg me pardon,
For stealing what I think not worth a fardon,
For he who stole the Calf, would steal the Cow,
If how alsewell to carry her off he knew;
Which makes me sorry you should thus your muse
Not Crimes to lash, but them defend; abuse:
For Poets, words not things, at pleasure use,
Nor will I pardon on a bare Confession,
Till you have quite extinguish'd your Transgression,
By fourfold Restitution, or by getting
A Renunciation from old *Tom* in writing,
Which, if he take advice, he'll not deny,
For I am sure he's sinn'd the self same way,
To that degree, that four-fold Restoration
Would make him far the poorest of the Nation,
These are the Terms on which I'll give Remission,
So that you might have spar'd your bare Submission

Sir,
I Remain (as you deserve) to Power,
You and all Robbers to suppress Balfour.

P. S.
See your Return be satisfieing,
Without one word therein of Lying,
Or else be sure with all my Pith,
I'll help to hang thee *Robie Smith.*

Mr.

Mr. *Robert Smith's* Rep[ly] *to Balfour.*

SIr yours informs me ye did mine receive,
By which you say I did your pardon crave,
Which I did not; but only made Confession
To you, and all, tho' small was my Transgression,
My Crime was small, your Clemency was less,
That would not pardon when I did confess.
　　Sir, you deny me what I never sought;
Why should I pardon beg of you for nought?
Against you I was not a Criminal,
Yea had I been, your Mercy had been small.
I truely think I had not got your pardon,
Although my Crime be no more than a farden,
Nor is it like I would steal Cow or Calf,
Hide well, deny, of theft is the best half,
I of my Crime did unrequir'd confess,
This shows I'm willing to make a Redress.
Nor yet did I abuse my Muse nor Rhyms,
Confession is a lash severe for Crimes,
When seconded with a firm Resolution,
To make the Les'd a four-fold Restitution.
You Prize my sang not to be worth a farden,
Then sure a pennie may purchase my pardon,
From *Tom* I'll seek no writ, nor will I scruple,
Instanter for to pay him the Quadruple,
Since I to him am now four farthings due,
I'll pay him and no pardon seek of you,
This shows my Crimes are neither great nor many
When by the Law my pardon's but a penny:
Suppress all Rogues and Robbers with your might,
I fear not when four farthings keeps my right.
　　　　The Truth I've told you without Lying,
　　　　Not fearing threats of Crucifying.
　　I'm sorry (Sir) that you should chuse,
So base a Trade to gain my Cloaths,

O　　　　　　　　　　　　　　　Al-

Although they have been worn long,
They're worth a hunder of my sang,
But if ye rax me limb and lith,
Then take the Coat of *Robie Smith.*
     July, *Glenshee* the fourteenth day,
     I got the Reply and gave Duply,   1710.

A Reply to the foregoing, Directed thus. *To Mr.*
Robert Smith *Schoolmaster in* Glenshee.

SIR, *July* the fourteenth I receiv'd your Letter,
  With a Duply, but the Reply was better ;
For good Sir, you must all sense abandon,
If to confess guilt be not to crave pardon,
You say your Crime was small, but understand
That who in one, doth fail in each Command :
And do not think altho' you did confess,
That e're Confession doth make guilt the less,
And whereas you my Clemency abuse,
To Thiefs I never Clemency shall use,
Since they by Laws both Civil and Divine,
To Death are adjudged for that shameless Crime.
You say that I deny'd what you ne'r sought,
Pardon to wit, pardon's not got for nought
By Criminals, the reason's good I'll swear,
Who Snuff-mills steals, would not an Ox forbear ;
If you design your Crimes for to redress,
You must your self in other Terms express,
And do not think by your Terms of Solution,
The Government's content with Restitution ;
I'm sure you should have known far better things,
For Thieves were hang'd with the King of Kings,
But since your Guilt you freely do confess,
If not crave pardon, then you do transgress :
Sir, you crave not my pardon, I'm not Pope,
But if I am, then you deserve a Rope   In-

Instanter, Theft without a farder scruple
Gibbet deserves, thee should with a quadruple,
I quarrel not your Crimes, tho' they be great,
No finite measure can your Crimes abate,
Your penny Theft tho' you account it small,
Your Soul, your Honour must account for all,
And tho' to *Tom* you satisfaction gave
Yet from our Laws they cannot you reprive,
But you must still our Sovereign's Laws obey,
In direct Terms who steals, high hang'd be they.
    I in sincerity and truth,
    Have sent by Letter not by Mouth,
    An Answer to your frivolous Rhyme,
    The Product not of thought but time,
    Your breeding doth you much expose,
    Which Ridiculs you not 'mongst foes,
    But Friends ; Sir after you got Sentence
    Of Death, you will come to Repentance
    I hope, and then within an hour,
    You'll Pardon get from good *Balfour*,
    Who to your Cloaths had no pretence,
    Though this appears your last Defence,
    For he who hath the power to hang
    Scorns Cloaths, tho he take the sang,
    Now take this Answer if you please,
    And let *Balfour* now dwell at ease ;
    Restore, amend with all your pith,
    And I'm your Servant *Robie Smith.*

    SIR, I will no more allow my Name to forge,
But plainly tell the Author's Nam's Ms *George*
Wishart, who lives in Town where every house is
Famous, e'r for Bellona or the Muses,
For Drinking, Fighting, or for wittie scribbling,
I leave it Sir to you to say, or quibbling,

But

But I remain I do you well assure,
You and your Muse still to admire *Balfour,*
Nor only pardon, but with all my pith,
Sends you my humble service ; *Robie Smith.*

*The Answer to the forgoing by Mr. Smith, Directed
thus.*

Unto the care of good *Balfour,*
I do commit the same,
That he may send't within an hour
Unto the Fox that yet doth lowr
Of Poetry for all his Pow'r,
He still conceals his Name,
Unto the care of kind *Balfour,*
I do commit the same.

SIR, all the blotts and scribblings of your Pen,
I've had the patience to peruse again,
In which I find, you guilty are of Crimes,
Which will you make the Scorn of future times.
In the first place, you love to lurk and low'r,
And Arrogats the Title of *Balfour,*
The Cloak was good, but he no Knaves will cover,
Because of such, he never was a lover.
Again thou shows thy stupid Ignorance,
In venting Lies thy Pillar and Defence,
For in thy first thou said, I beg'd thy pardon,
Which I esteem far less, than half a farden,
Had thou at first read mine aright, thou'd found,
Thy own assertion built on sandy ground.
Sir to your self, I pray you be so kind }
To read aright, consider, and you'll find, }
Your gross mistakes, or sure I am you'r blind. }
Will you consider your own Lies and Fictions,
Your skill in Law, and obvious contradictions
                                        There-

Therefore I'll instance some lines of your Letter,
To show all Men your pure nonsense the better,
Now all who reads this, give a shout and hallow ;
His contradictions and nonsense doth follow.
" Nor will I pardon on a bare Confession, (sion
" Till you have quite extinguish'd your Transgres-
" by fourfold Restitution, or by getting
" A Renunciation from Old *Tom* in Writing :
" If you design your Crimes for to redress,
" you must yourself in other Terms express,
" And do not think by your Terms of Solution,
" The Government's content with Restitution.
 These are your words, let any Man of sense
Hear what you can say in your own defence,
Here you confest that fourfold Restitution,
The fault extinguish'd and got Absolution :
Had you held here, you had the rightest Cause ;
Because it was an Act of Divine Laws.
But oh ! From them I see you to dissent, ⎫
Because it does not please the Government, ⎬
I'm sorry you should so base Tenets vent. ⎭
 I for my Crime did Restitution make,
I'll keep no Laws of Men Gods Laws to break ;
You say, that no Confession guilt makes less,
But (Sir) the Scriptures bids us all confess,
Confession is the way for to forsake,
But I regrate you for your gross mistake,
I did confess, forsook, and so I hope,
No Laws of Men can judge me to a Rope,
The Penitent thou knows he Mercy got,
Or if thou knows not, sure thou're but a sot,
Balfour and *Tom* they both have pardon'd me,
And thou may see they both think shame of thee ;
Thou guilty art of Forgery and Lies,
'Tis for such Crimes that thou thy Name denys
       Thou

Thou writes my name thy nonsense to decore,
As thou a better fellows wrote before,
To wit *Balfour's ;* how ill becam't thy station,
For to commit so high an Usurpation ?
   I see indeed you're very fain to hang,
And get my Cloaths for one poor farthings sang,
Because thou'rt fear'd for Dying on a Tree,
To be the Hang-man you have chois'd I see,
And rather hang, than for to hanged be,
Because by no means else you can pass free,
Therefore thou crys that sentence soon may pass,
Ear's are not *Horns*, who need's fear the Ass,
Tho they be long they've neither strength nor pith
No more has all your threats to *Robie Smith.*

    S I R,
   What means that nonsense in your Rhyme,
The Product not of thought but time,
To every one who doth it hear,
Thou makes thy Ignorance appear,
And all do judge that *Bacchus* Oyl
Thy Brain confused all this while.
Fall on again and mend thy Pen,
And scour the Barm from off thy Brain,
Learn to write with fewer blotts,
Lest some should think all Poets Sots.
And spell some better if thou can,
Or else consult some other Man,
If thou would rightly Poetize,
Be sure a Capital to use
In the beginning of each Line,
Or when thou writs look ay to mine ;
To write the next take some less time,
Spend not so much on stinking Rhyme ;
Date thy Letters, write thy Name,
Or hold thy peace with scorn and shame,   And

And when I know you, I shall be
Still yours to serve you in *Glenshee*,
In each respect, as you do me,
Beat thy Brain, and try thy pith,
See if thou'll conquer *Robie Smith*.
    Glenshee November the Eight Day,
    I got and did the same Repay.   1710.

    Unto the Laird of Fefartie,
    Who is at present in Glenshee.

OF *Morpheus* Bonds most willingly
  This Day I did myself unty,
When I forsook him I heard all,
The Birds with Songs for Day to call,
Nights Sentinels were scarcely gone,
Nor had *Sol* view'd the *Horizon*,
When (Sir) I went to *Finningand*,
To Implement your kind command
In order to get Nets and Dogs,
To hunt wild Beasts through Heaths and Bogs.
He told me that his Dog was tyr'd,
Nor yet could he be lent nor hir'd,
Therefore my Labour proved vain,
And I came empty back again.
  Sir, Join all your Arratisms
With Sophistrie and Syllogisms;
And let Ms *John Meanders* hatch,
And try what Venison he'll catch,
And use his utmost witt and skill,
Red Deer, Murchens, and Tods to kill,
Which he may use more Innocent,
Than he Collects the Bishops Rent,
Sir, I am yours at your Command,
Robert Smith with heart and hand.

                             To

To the Tune of Allan-water.   *New Lines.*

THere's nothing but thy cold disdain,
  Shall ever make my Love abated,
But if thou Love not me again
I'll scorn thy Love, if mine be hated,
The Muses then shall all aggree.
And mount my Soul unto *Parnassus*
From *Venus* and *Cupid* I'll be free,
And from the Cares of the finest Lasses.

2.
Shall I thee Love, tho' thou me hate,
No, no, I'll scorn such a silly passion,
Or be induc'd for to intreat,
For Pity where there's no Compassion,
I'll sooner break all *Cupids* Darts,
And *Venus* Bonds all Rend assunder,
And cast their care from off my Heart,
And still disdain to ly beyond her.

3.
I by my Pen and hands can live,
In Honesty and Comely Honour,
Let Blockheads who wants Spirits grieve
If she frowns I'll not dote upon her.
But 'tis for thy lyking I thee Love,
These are the Chains that still doth bind me,
If equal Charms thy heart doth move,
Thou kind and constant still shall find me.

4.
But if thou chance for to neglect
And slight the scorching flames that move me,
I Swear that I'll thee dissaffect,
And wish much joy to all who loves thee.
Yet had I Diadems and Crowns,
And Kingdoms I'd bestow them on thee,

                                    But

But if I chance to fell thy frowns.
I Swear my fancy shall flee from thee.

The Lass her Reply 2d part to the same Tune.

MY dearest dear what would I give,
To be in sure possession of thee,
Though all the Worlds vast round were mine,
I'd be content to give it for thee.
Were the Mountains, Hills and Rocks all Gold,
And all the stones an heap of treasure,
Yet I would chuse thy self to be
My Portion, O sweet Soul of pleasure.

2.

Alas thy frowns wou'd afford more grief,
Than all the Joys that these could give me,
Oh ! For the hardness of thy heart,
Still saying, thou does not believe me ;
All day thou lys nearest my heart,
And that in spight of opposition,
O may the Powers above impart,
Some pity to my sad condition.

3.

In hopes that I may ease my grief,
I sing and sport sometime for fashion,
Yet all alas brings no relief,
But serves to aggravate my passion.
A Bed which is a sweet repose,
And where each one soft sleep embraces,
All night I tumble there and toss
Thy sweet *Idea* me so traces.

4.

Then if mine eyes but chance to close
Then presently my Soul flys to thee,
'Tis then I have my best repose,
By fancying that I still am with thee,

P   But

But when I awake and find thou'rt gone,
O then my Soul is fill'd with sorrow,
With Sighings sad I lay me down,
Longing for the approaching morrow.

5.

Chuse whom thou will, she's never have
The veneration I have for thee,
Who willingly would all things leave,
And be or do what thou would have me :
But if my sute thou do refuse,
All after Ages shall abhore thee,
And curse thy Name and thee abuse
For slighting her, who so ador'd thee.

6.

No ancient story can relate
An instance of such admiration ;
Or one whose Love was e're so great
That ever mist of a Compensation :
Therefore I hope that thou will be,
No precedent to things ungratful,
And O sweet Heavens forbid to me,
That ever thou cause thy name be hateful.

7.

Yea had I Diadems and Crowns,
And Kingdoms I'd bestow them on thee ;
But oh ! I fear I'll fell thy frowns,
Because my fancy's fixed on thee :
But still I hope sweet *Venus* will,
With *Cupid* keep thee from such error,
And wound thy heart, since thou did kill
My heart and Soul with Love and Terror.

8.

Yea sure I am if thou knew my grief,
And had the heart of a Human Creature,
Thou could not miss to give relief,
And carry some part of my sad fetter :   Now

Now here I'll end with this request,
That kind Heaven would be pleas'd to move thee;
And fix a flame within thy Breast,
That thou may know so Dear's I Love thee.

Upon an excellent young Lady Mrs. Margaret C.
by Ro. Smith.   Extempore.

HEr Beauty all Men do admire,
 Her Vertue sets all Hearts on fire,
Her Worth and Merits doth excel,
All that all mortal Tongues can tell:
For all who see her must confess,
She's full of Beauty, Witt and Grace;
This Paragon shall ever be
Admir'd by me continually.

The young Lady's Answer   Extempore.
YOur Verses flow in such a stream
 Of Virtues, that I cannot claim,
But I discharge that e're my name
Ye should venture to proclaim.
For good or bad I'd take it ill,
That on me ye should try your skill
Of Poesy, but writ your fill,
Upon *Balfour* his Snichen-Mill.

An other Elogy to the Lady by R. S. Extempore.
MAdam, my strains are all too low to show,
 The worthy praise that to your Merite's due:
For I in verse did not your Name Proclaim,
For *Ovid* it would be a Meeter Theme,
And yet his skill could never set you forth,
Nor show the Thousand part of your true worth.
If *Adam* had been bless'd with such a Wife,
He had continu'd in the state of Life
                    P 2   In

In you all Vertue primitively shine ;
You'r a Compend of all that is Divine ;
Heroick Vertues dwells within your Breast,
Where Meekness doth with Greatness still contest.
Would *Pallas, Juno, Venus,* once again
Strive for the *Palm* in *Idas* shaddy plain,
If you were there, then all these Goddesses
Would yield to you for Beauty, Witt & Grace ;
Had *Paris* but your Lovely Beauty seen,
Then he'd disdain'd fair *Helena* the Queen :
Each one in you might find far greater Joy,
Than in her Face, for whom he burnt his Troy ;
Your Words and Actions all compleat with Grace,
And Paradice is painted in your Face.
Yea sure I am, were *Adam's* Off-spring all
Like unto you, I'd swear ther'd been no fall.
Now to conclude, I solemnly Protest
All Pandors Gifts in you the Gods have plac'd.

Directed thus.

To her whose Beauty all admire,
And Vertue sets all Hearts on fire,
Of whom I swear in all respects,
She is the Phœnix of her Sex,
To her alone I write this Theme,
Who is of Beauty Diademe.

The Lady's 2d Reply   Extempore.

THis Morning I happened for to see
    Some Verses full of Rhapsodie,
Written as I do suppose,
By one who fast to Bedlame goes.
Is *Vulcan* now become a Poet ?
It's like he will prove a great Stoick,
And crack his Brain with Nonsense Rhyme,
I think his Lightness be his Crime.   Ro.

Ro. Smith's *Reply to the former* Extempore.

IF I be he whom you suppose,
That so fast unto Bedlam goes,
How soon so ever I come there,
Some room for you I shall prepare :
If it be Rhymes that makes me light,
It is a Gemm which makes you bright ;
Since it doth with your Virtues join,
Above your Sex it makes you shine,
I'm happy thrice in all respects,
Since what's my Vice, can grace your Sex.

To the Earl of Kinnoul, *October* 28*th*, 1713.

MAy't please your Lordship for to know,
That I came here a year ago,
And had a Precept from *Pitmedden,*
For Rents to Bishops now forbidden :
O woe be to that cursed Coin
Was taken from those Men Divine,
And given to arrant Cheats and Fools,
And Dominies for teaching Schools.
To won't we beat our Brains and Lungs,
We tire our Spirits and our Tongues,
We waste our strength, our Limbs we tire,
And seeking't wades through Dub and Mire,
We're sent from hand to hand like Fools,
Which makes us to neglect our Schools :
They set us by with shams and shifts,
They love so well King *William's* Gifts.
The little good that's done, we do it,
And cannot get what is allow'd.
Tho Bees do toil, Drons eat the Honey,
The Worlds Hearts are join'd to Money :
But Noble Earl, I have got from you,
What sticks to others Hearts like Glew,   My

My Lord I hope you'll not Repent,
And what remains you'll Implement :
And while I live, or keep a School,
I shall still pray for good *Kinnoul*,
My Lord I'm yours with all my Pith,
To serve your Lordship *Robert Smith.*

An E L E G I E, *Upon the never enough to be La-
mented Death of the Illustrious and Noble* JOHN
Marquess of Tullibardine, *who departed this Life
at the Battle near* Mons *the first of* September,
1709.

WHat Sighs, what Groans are these I hear always?
  What gushing Torrents now run from all Eyes?
What woful News? What killing sound is this,
That fills all Hearts with Grief and Bitterness?
Ah! Doleful News! But they cannot be fled,
The *Noble Marquess Tullibardine's Dead.*
That *Sweet*, that *Noble Matchless Paragon*,
Ah! Is he gone? He's gone, Alas he's gone.
What Eyes do not with Mournful Tears run down?
What Heart's not struck with this (Death-striking)
          sound?
Ah! Cruel Death! Could nought thy Hunger fill?
But must thou *Noble Tullibardine* Kill:
Could nothing serve to satiate thy greed,
But must thou glut thy self in's Noble Blood?
All Tongues, all Pens cannot aright descry
The matchless worth of him thou's ta'en away.
His Noble Soul was Vertues real seat,
And Vertue made his Soul with Grace compleat;
Ignoble Deeds in him bore never sway :
His Fame will stand before Black-Mouth'd Envy.
For Courage *Ajax*, *Hector*, *Alexander*,
A Loyal Subject and a brave Commander.
In Eloquence he second was to none ;
And he for Beauty was an *Absolom*

For Wisdom he did far his Age excel.
But why should I his praise attempt to tell,
I'd hold the Seas far sooner in my hand,
And without Pen or Ink recount the sand,
Or weigh the Earth in an Imponderous scale,
Far sooner than his worthy Merits tell.
His Trump of Fame shall the wide World hear,
And his good Name all Monuments outwear:
No Marble Tomb or Trophee's Virtue needs,
Fame is his Herauld and proclaims his Deeds.
His Praises fill Ten Thousand Thousand Mouths,
He was the Mirror of all Noble Youths:
But now alas! Grim Death hath him assail'd;
Belov'd he liv'd by all, and dyed bewail'd.
His Warfare is ended, and his Peace begun,
All Storms are past, and he enjoys the Sun;
Corruption Incorruption hath put on;
He's gone from Earth unto an Heavenly Throne.
Where he shall have an everlasting Crown
Of Glory, Joy, of Peace and High Renoun.

An ELEGIE, *Upon the never enough to be La-*
mented Death of the Illustrious *and* Noble PA-
TRICK Lord Glames, *who departed this Life*
  the   *Day of*   1709.

HOw vainly vain are sublunary things? (Kings?
How great's Deaths Pow'r, the Conqueror of
By which he brings all living to the Dust,
The High, the Low, the Wicked and the Just.
No Prince, nor Peer can claim Immunity,
No Birth, no Breeding nor high Quality
Can be exeem'd from Deaths Tyrannick Rage:
All must with Death once in this War engage,
And feel the stroke of his o'recoming hand.
Since *Noble Glames* is gone at his Command; How

How many Eyes salt Brinnish Tears do shed
For him? who now is grim Death's Captive made.
Brave *Glams* is gone, who was both good & great,
A lively swatch of Mans Primeve State:
Whose budding leaves did of such odour smell,
As did his Age, his Rank, his Sex excell;
Heroick Vertue dwelt within his Breast,
Where meekness did with greatness still contest;
And 'tis uncertain which did bear the sway,
Virtuous greatness or Humility:
A Judge Impartial with most curious Eye,
To none could Judge the prize of Victory.
In him the Lyon and the Lamb did join,
And both did show rare Qualities Divine:
Majestick Courage from the one did flow,
Pure Innocence did with the other grow,
And so well mixt that each one must declare,
That both of them did claim an equal share,
Pure Gold from Dross, pure Silver purg'd from Tin,
Without unspotted, Innocent within.
No boiling passions could his Soul molest,
Because it was with Virtue prepossest.
In him all Gifts and Graces were in store,
That could a *Hero* or a Soul decore,
The Rose and Lillie strove who should take place,
To paint their Colours in his Noble Face.
The one did not unto the other yield,
But both did dwell upon this Heavenly field,
And did their Colours in such sort display,
That Paradice was open to each Eye
For Beauty; and for Eloquence and Strain,
He was a noble *Cicero* again.
Yea such Endowments he enjoy'd them all,
That Men could good, or Women pleasant call:
But Earthly Joys which all do most desire,
Ah! Ah! Alas! They soonest do expire.

So

So this pure Rose, Alas! was soon cut down
Before of's worth the Thousand part was known,
But stay my Muse unfit for such a Task,
For fear that thou his splendid Praises mask
By thy harsh Notes, gross sense, unpollisht Brains;
Too high a Subject for Ten Thousand Pens ;
Return, Return, his Noble Soul is gone,
From's Earthly Palace to an Heavenly Throne,
With those Palm-bearing Companys to be
On *Zions* Mount throughout Eternity.
To love his Creator and his King adore,
And Bath in Bless and Joy for evermore.

To the Memory of Lachlan M'pherson, *who departed this Life the   day of   1708.
(breath

HOw short's Life's date? And ah! How soon's our
Evapourate, and we crush'd down by Death ?
Death, whose devouring Pow'r none can withstand
Nor shun the stroke of his o'ercoming hand,
Hath now led captive *One* from off the stage,
A Paragon of worth, who did engage
All Hearts to Love him, and his Loss Lament:
But Ah! Alas! Who can Deaths Pow'r prevent?
Had Birth, had breeding claim'd Immunitie,
Than he from Death had been exeem'd and free.
But Ah! Alas! There's nothing here that can,
Exeem us from the common Lot of Man.
The Gifts of Grace and Nature all did meet
In him, to make a Man and Saint compleat:
Mild as the Lamb, and harmless as the Dove,
Yea Beautys Mirror, and the Soul of Love.
His Colour like the Milk well mixt with Wine,
The Rose and Lillie in his Face did shine,
And so well mixt that it were hard to tell,
Which of the Two the other did excell:

Q   In

In him were all the Gifts, that could or can
Make up a Generous, Gentle, Pretty Man.
As Natures Gifts were on his Body plac'd,
So Divine Grace his Heavenly Soul had grac'd ;
Yea all the Gifts in him made their abodes,
That *Pandor* had received from the gods.
But as the Flow'rs that all the rest excells
In Colour, and in Odouriferous smells,
Are soonest pluckt ! Ah ! So was he cut down
By cruel Death, before his Worth was known.
What faults he had, (for who from Faults are free)
He did bewail with deep Humilitie.
On Wings of Faith his Soul's ascended high,
And mounted up through the Stelliferous Sky,
Where now he triumphs, and *Zions* Songs doth sing,
In Praises to God his Father and his King.

To the Memory of Alexander Ferguson *of* Bruch-
　derger,* *who departed this Life the* 15 *of* February,
　1710.

HOw vainly vain is all below the Sun ? (run ?
　How shorts Life's Race? And ah? How quickly
What multitude of dang'rous Evils attend
Our way, to this uncertain Journeys end.
Yet still we fly on hastning wings, as posts ;
Throw all those Evils to Eternal Coasts :
Alas ! The living seldom lays to heart,
The conquering Pow'r of Deaths o'ercoming dart,
From which no living great or small can be
Exeem'd or spared from his Tyrannie ;
To Deaths pale scepter all must Tribute pay,
He's King o'er all and doth the Scepter sway :
To Death all Monarchs must resign the Crown,
And Conquering *Heroe's* lay their Glory down
　　　　　　　　　　　　　　　　　　The

* [Farquharson of Bruchderg *in the Index.*]

The Nobles greatness, no nor Birth can save,
Nor keep them from the all devouring Grave.
He who's now gone, I think might been exeem'd,
Were any of his rank or sex redeem'd,
From Deaths devouring all o'recoming hand,
The Conqueror of all by Sea and Land.
Lament *Glenshee* your Ornament is gone;
Let all *Glenegla* sable weed put on;
And let each one for him Lament apart,
Who is remov'd by Death's Impartial Dart.
Alas! He's gone, who well deserv'd to be
Renown'd for Courage and Humilitie;
Sweet, Meek and Lowly, keeping peace with care,
And yet his Courage did out-face dispair,
No wounding Weapons could him terrify,
Nor Lawless Rascals could they make him fly,
He chuse far rather than his Friends forsake,
To paun his Life and pledge it at the stake,
He lov'd his Country and his Neighbours so,
That for their sakes he could his Life bestow.
  His Courage knew not what it was to yield,
Nor could his foot e're retrograd the field;
His Enemies must either from him fly,
Or else resolve in Blood or Gore to dy;
When show'rs of Balls thick as the Hail did fly,
And Guns were roaring like the thundering Sky,
Unterrified, and unaffrighted He
Behav'd himself with Magnanimitie,
And did his Foes confound and put to shame,
And to himself obtained a lasting Name
Of Virtue, Praise, which time cannot deface,
Nor can Envy e're make his glory less:
Whom Balls, nor Swords, nor Foes could overthrow,
Alas! Grim Death hath now reduc'd him low,
In Peace and rest he dy'd In's House at home,
And his good name supplys a Marble Tomb.

Through

Through many storms and broils, he's gain'd the
Of lasting Peace and Joy for evermore :   (shore
He loved Peace, Tranquillity and Rest,
And now of them he wholly is possest.

To the Memory of James Hog, *Laird of* Remore,
  Who departed this Life the   day of
                              (plext ?

WHo hath the Heart that's not with grief per-
  Or who the Soul that's not with Sorrow vext?
For him now gone, by Death's impartial blow ;
He was dear lov'd by all who did him know.
O Cruel Death ! Where Life is lov'd thou kills ;
But where it's loath'd, thou will not work their
In kindness he to all was like a Brother, (wills.
And tender hearted as a Loving Mother,
To all in want ; and did their Needs supply :
He's gone ; alas ! How many Tongues may say ?
He did increase his Fortune by his pain,
But hated every base and sinful gain :
Fraud, Guile, Deceit, great care he took to shun,
And what he did, was done before the Sun :
His Deeds were all with Grace and Virtue crown'd,
And in all Ears made a Melodious sound.
His Pious Soul did *Jacob's* Ladder scanse,
Because above he had's Inheritance.
Constant he was, and still he took great care
His Soul to save, and for its rest prepare.
His panting Soul long'd as a Bird in Cage,
For to pass off from this terrestrial Stage,
And be with him in whom all Joys are found,
That he for ever might his Praises sound,
Among these Triumphant Companys above,
Where Christ himself is all their Light and Love.
Of what he most desir'd, He's now possest,
His Soul's to God, his Body's gone to rest.   Ye

Ye Pious Souls for him be no more sorry,
Bear with your Loss, for he enjoyeth Glory.

To the Memory of Mr. Hary Forbes, Son *to* Mr. Jo.
  Forbes *Parson of* Kincardinonil, *who departed
  this Life the   Day of*

HOw many Souls feels grief, and Eyes do tear,
  For the bright Star now plucked from the
    Sphear?
Oh! Woes me for the Rose thats now cut down
By Deaths sharp scyth, before its worth was known
Whose budding leaves did odours sweet forth send,
Ay more belov'd the more it did extend.
He's gone, alas! Regrated is by all,
That such a flower hath had so quick a fall.
He was but show'n upon this Earthly stage,
By's youth to teach those of far greater age.
Wit, Love and Grace his Life they did decore,
Who knew him once, desir'd to know him more,
He modest was, Religious, Just and Kind,
Sprightful in Person, of a generous mind,
The hurtful passions, in youth that often Reigns,
He did repress, by clipping off the Wings
Of Pride, Ambition, Hate, Envy and Lust,
Still making God his only stay and trust.
If in the blossom he did smell so sweet;
What had he done, if come to riper Fruit?
As his pure Soul came down from God above,
It still ascended back again by Love:
He as an Eagle soared still on high,
Upon the Wings of sacred Extasy.
His Soul is landed on Emmanuals shore:
No Tumbling Billows shall affright him more,
He's now at rest, and to his God doth sing
Sweet songs of Praise unto his Prince and King.
                                              To

To the Memory of Margaret Rattray *Lady of* Bleaton *who departed this Life the* 7 *of* January 1710.

O Terrible and all subdueing Death !
Which Conquers all that draweth vital breath,
How many Souls are now in Sorrows clade
For her, whom thou haste with thee Captive led?
Where Life is lov'd, thou readiest art to kill,
Thou takes the good, but longest spares the ill ;
She who's now gone by thy impartial blow,
Was dearly lov'd by all who did her know.
Her Actions all became a generous mind,
And indicate her Genious refin'd,
No hurtful passion in her breast found rest,
Her Generous Soul with Virtue was possest.
Of Gifts and Graces, all she had in store,
That could a Body or a Soul decore.
Earth she esteem'd not her Inheritance,
(To higher aims her Soul did still advance)
The thing which made her herein pleasure take,
Was only for her Spouse and Childrens sake ;
To whom she show'd all duty and respect :
Yea, she to none her Duty did neglect.
A gesture grave she had, a temper free
Of Impudence, and dull Morositie ;
Which did unto the World at large set forth,
Her to be one of true and real worth ;
Therefore her Saviour saw her fit to be
Remov'd from Sorrows to Felicity,
He's call'd her home unto himself by Death,
Because she was more fit for Heaven than Earth,
She's now at rest, free from the frowns of fate,
Her Soul enjoys a blest Immortal state :
She's now gone to those Mansions above,
To Praise her God, her King, her Joy, her Love.

A

A Poem.

WHy should vain Man this wretched World
        regard?
Since all its Comforts fades like *Jonahs* Gourd
Tho to his Soul at first it gave delight,
It soon was gone and wither'd with the Night.
   Fortun's unconstant, all the World must own,
No King's secure on the best fixed Throne.
What's frothy Honour? but the Vulgars breath,
Bestowed on poor sinful Lumps of Earth.
Increase of Riches brings increase of trouble,
Increase of Knowledge makes our Sorrows double.
And by experience we daily find,
Our surest Friends inconstant as the wind.
One's Rich to day, to morrow he's as poor,
This day she's modest, but the next a Whore;
This hour something above our Souls we prize,
The next we do them thrice as much despise;
What this day is the object of our Love,
Does of our hate again the Object prove;
In what this year we sweetest pleasure take,
The next we'll loath, and it again forsake:
What past for Virtue in the former times,
Is held for Vice and punished for Crimes.
Why should we dote on any thing so vain,
As paints it self with pleasure or with gain;
And cannot give the Soul its full content,
And are but vainly vain, when off's the paint:
Yea Follies mingled with our Words and Actions,
And all our Thoughts are meerly but Distractions,
Which fills our Souls with horrid Perturbation,
And proves all vain and only Souls Vexation.
We spend our time in courting foolish Toys,
We marry Sorrows in the place of Joys.   Now

Now then my Soul since nothing's constant here,
Hoise up thy Sails, weigh Anchor, and go stear
Another course; make haste, streatch out thy Sails,
And Heaven invock to lend thee prosperous gales
To waft thee over to Emmanuels shore,
To bath in bliss, and joy for ever more.
Let not the dangers which may seem to be
Into thy way, at all discourage thee:
Tho' winds blow lowdly and the Tide be high,
Tho' foamy billows beat thy Vessels side,
And tho thy flesh and blood begin to chide,
Why should thou fear, thou hast a skilful guide,
Who thousand Souls has wafted ov'r before,
And set them safe upon the wisht for shore.
When Tempests roars and Winds are contrar,
Then fix thine eye on the bright Morning Star,
And let thy Soul be ravish'd with his Light,
And then no Clouds of darkness will affright,
With gloominess, or make thee loss thy way,
His darkest Clouds are clearer than noon-day.
But if a Cloud shall chance to interpose,
And raise thy fears, for fear thy way thou lose,
Then on the sacred Compass let thine eye
Be fixt, and it will all again display,
Then let thy Sails of hope again be spread,
Till thou win o'er thy discontenting dread:
If flesh and blood would wish thee to return,
Show forth the danger how you both must burn
In endless wrath without remeed or ease,
Therefore beware strive not thy flesh to please,
But crucify whatever would gainstand
Thy Prosperous Voyage to Emmanuels Land,
Fly from the monsters which are in the main,
Which would affright thee to return again.
O! Let thy heart and thy affection be
On thy dear Friend, who looks and longs for thee,
And

And shall thee with his Lovely Arms embrace,
And wipe the Tears & Sweat from thy blurr'd face;
And Crown thee with an everlasting Crown,
And on a Throne of Glory set thee down.
Now Joy begins, and all our Griefs are gone,
When we'll enjoy Heavens matchless Paragon :
This will our Toil and Labour Recompence,
We'll have a Joy cannot be known by sense.
Their Friends cannot deceive us, nor annoy
Our quiet rest, nor break our solid Joy ;
Their Sorrows shall not interrupt our rest,
But shall in all we do, see, hear, be blest.
Our Gourd of Bliss shall then for ever spring,
It's Loss will then no discontentment bring,
But in its shade we shall for ever be
Refresh'd, delighted to Eternitie :
Soon come that Day when we shall be possest,
Into this sweet this happy Heavenly Rest.

Soli DEO Gloria.

Lines made on a Christmas Morning.

LEt *Zion's* Sons and Daughters all
　Rejoice exceedingly,
All that was lost by *Adam's* fall,
It is restor'd this Day :
Let Heaven and Earth, and all rejoice,
For this Days Blessed Birth :
Because *Emmanuel* did chose,
To come from Heaven to Earth,
That He the Captives might set free,
Who by their Sins were dead,
He did procure their Libertie,
And bruise the Serpents head.
Upon the Earth this Day he did
In humble form appear,

R　　　　　　　　　Tho'

Tho' Him the Earthy Fools deride,
The Devils quake and fear :
And all the Sons of God did sing,
High Praises to the Name
Of this blest Babe, and Heavenly King,
Now Born in *Bethlehem.*
The Angels did like swift wing'd fire
Fly and the Shepherds tell,
That of all Nations the Desire
Is born, *Emmanuel.*
Therefore let all both great and small,
Extoll this blessed Birth
With Heavenly Voice : let all rejoice,
And tremble with your Mirth.

A Wish.

O! That I could thy Lofty Name so praise,
  As thou deserves ; if I my voice could raise
Above the Heavens, and the loud tongu'd thunder,
And still proclaim thy works so full of wonder.
O ! May my Soul for ever be in fire
Of Love to thee, and more and more desire
To do thy will while I am here below ;
And for this end, O Lord thy Grace bestow.
My heart is hard, Lord break the rock of Flint,
And grant I may of all my sins Repent.
Wo's me poor wretch, I've play'd the Prodigal,
I've run from thee, though thou did often call
Me to return : Yet I thy voice Divine
Have slighted still, and fed on Husks with Swine.
  Grant now O Lord ! I may return with speed;
And Mercy beg according to my need :
From Thee, and Thee alone I Mercy crave,
Not as a Son, but as a wretched slave.

Since

Since in Thy House is Bread enough to spare.
Out of Thy Mercy, let me have a share :
A Crumb from Thy rich Table will supply
My fainting Soul, which ready is to die,
Thou freely gives, Lord I have nought can buy;
I plead for Mercy to my Misery.
Thy Fountains full, thy Mercy knows no bounds,
Apply a Balsom to my Blooding Wounds.
O ! Save my Soul, and do my Blooding stem,
And take the Praise and Glory to Thy Name.

F I N I S.

[*To* William Seton *younger of* Pitmedden,
*who has the Management of the Bishop Rents
of* Dunkeld, *and some others.*

MUch Honoured Sir, I here return [to] you,
My Hearty Thanks, yea, and good Wishes too;
For sending here my Money to my Door,
And for too seek it troubled me no more.
Each one gets from you whats to them Assign'd,
Yea, 'tis your very Nature to be kind.
To have you still, till Bishops be Restor'd,
Is what's by me and all the rest Implor'd.
'Tis you and such deserves the Publick Trust,
Whose Conscience and whose Dealings are so just.
O may kind Heaven you, and all such preserve,
Who from what's Right loves never for to swerve.
Sir, I am yours with greater will than pith,
To serve your Honour, while I'm
　　　　　　　　　　　Robie Smith.
Glenshee, Nov :
　1714. [1713].

F I N I S.]

INDEX,

Part 2d.

Upon

I N D E X.

I N D E X.

F I N I S.

www.ingramcontent.com/pod-product-compliance
Lightning Source LLC
Chambersburg PA
CBHW030904050726
47500CB00009B/1019